The Secret of Skeleton Reef

Joe turned. In the distance he saw the protruding dorsal fins of three sharks. "It's okay," he said to Frank. "I came face-to-face with a shark when I was diving earlier. He didn't bother me at all. Apparently they're mostly dangerous to humans if the humans are near the shore or if the humans are—"

"What is it?" Frank asked, seeing a stunned look on Joe's face.

"One of us is bleeding," Joe said seriously.

Frank glimpsed a trail of crimson blood in the clear water. "Oh, no," he said. "It must be the cut I got from the anchor line. The water probably pulled off my bandage and opened the wound."

Frank knew what Joe had been about to say before he saw the blood. Sharks were dangerous to humans only if the humans were near the shore—or if they were bleeding!

The Hardy Boys Mystery Stories

Available from MINSTREL Books

THE HARDY BOYS®

144

THE SECRET OF
SKELETON REEF

FRANKLIN W. DIXON

A MINSTREL® BOOK

Published by POCKET BOOKS
New York   London   Toronto   Sydney   Tokyo   Singapore

This book is a work of fiction. Names, characters, places and incidents are products of the author's imagination or are used fictitiously. Any resemblance to actual events or locales or persons, living or dead, is entirely coincidental.

A MINSTREL PAPERBACK *Original*

A Minstrel Book published by
POCKET BOOKS, a division of Simon & Schuster Inc.
1230 Avenue of the Americas, New York, NY 10020

Copyright © 1997 by Simon & Schuster Inc.

Front cover illustration by John Youssi

Produced by Mega-Books, Inc.

All rights reserved, including the right to reproduce
this book or portions thereof in any form whatsoever.
For information address Pocket Books, 1230 Avenue
of the Americas, New York, NY 10020

ISBN: 0-671-00056-X

First Minstrel Books printing June 1997

10 9 8 7 6 5 4 3 2 1

THE HARDY BOYS MYSTERY STORIES is a trademark
of Simon & Schuster Inc.

THE HARDY BOYS, A MINSTREL BOOK and colophon
are registered trademarks of Simon & Schuster Inc.

Printed in the U.S.A.

Contents

1 Tale of the Ghost

"Man, this is the life," Joe Hardy said as he nestled a bare foot into the powdery white beach sand. Glancing up, he saw a slender crescent moon glowing in the night sky.

Frank looked at his younger brother and said, "Get a clue, Joe. They don't say 'man' in the Caribbean. They say 'mon.' "

"Okay, mon," Joe said. "Don't sweat it."

"Don't worry, I won't," Frank said, leaning back in the sand, using his backpack as a pillow. "Working up a sweat is the last thing on my mind."

"Well, if anybody needs a little rest and recreation, it's Frank and Joe Hardy," Jamal Hawkins said. Jamal was a seventeen-year-old the Hardys had gotten to know on one of their cases. As luck would have it, Jamal's uncle owned a bungalow on the Caribbean island of St. Lucia, and Jamal had invited the Hardys to join him on the island for some summer fun in the sun.

The boys sat silently a few moments, enjoying the pleasantly warm Caribbean night. A faint breeze rustled through the fronds of the palm trees. The three had arrived on the island only two hours earlier and had wasted no time getting to the water.

The sea lapped gently several yards away. Frank felt himself becoming hypnotized by the slow, easy sound of the waves.

"Peaceful, isn't it?" Jamal said finally.

"You can say that again," Frank replied.

"You know, I like action more than anybody," Joe said, "but right now I'm really looking forward to a complete break from it all. No school, no chores, no life-threatening situations."

"I'll believe it when I see it," Jamal said. "If you ask me, you guys aren't even capable of relaxing. If there's trouble lurking anywhere in this part of the world, I know you guys are going to stumble into it." Jamal glanced at them with a knowing smile.

Both Hardys attended Bayport High School and occasionally slipped into the roles of teenage detectives. Frank Hardy was tall and had dark hair. At eighteen he was a year older than Joe, as well as an inch taller. Intelligent and even-tempered, Frank was seldom anybody's fool.

Blond Joe, on the other hand, was more the impulsive type. Though he was also smart, Joe sometimes allowed his emotions and instincts to guide his actions.

"Jamal, you're no stranger to danger yourself," Joe chided. "You got us into one of our scariest cases yet."

"True," Jamal admitted. "I just don't go looking for disaster the way you guys do."

Jamal was slender and a little shorter than the Hardys, but he could match either one in athletic ability. Jamal's father owned a commuter airline in Bayport, and Jamal was an expert pilot himself.

Hearing voices down the beach, Frank turned to see two young men approaching. They were both in their twenties and had the tanned, laid-back look of California surfers. Each had long hair, one blond, the other light brown.

"How's it going, guys?" the blond one said, stopping right by Jamal and the Hardys.

"Oh, not too shabby," Joe answered. "Just checking out the waves."

"Too bad you can't see what's underneath that water," the blond one said. By the accent, Frank could tell he was a fellow citizen of the U.S.

"What do you mean?" Frank asked.

"Sunken ships is what I mean," the blond replied. "There are plenty of wrecks out there, and I've seen tons of them. Everything from fishing boats to luxury yachts. There is a reef four miles offshore that's awfully dangerous to boats in bad weather."

"Hey," Jamal said, "we heard there were some treasure hunters stationed on the island. They're supposed to be searching for the remains of a sunken pirate ship. You guys wouldn't be a part of that scene, would you?"

The blond smiled slyly and hitched up his shorts. "We were trying to keep this thing quiet, but on a small island, word gets around eventually. As a matter of fact, we're members of the crew looking for that pirate ship. I'm Ted, and this is Dirk."

Frank noticed that Ted and Dirk looked pretty impressed with themselves as he introduced himself and Joe and Jamal.

"I guess a lot of pirates sailed these waters way back when, didn't they?" Joe asked.

"They sure did," Ted said, glancing out at the calm water of the Caribbean Sea. "Several hundred years ago the Spanish conquistadors were busy conquering South and Central America. They stole tons of precious metals and gems from the natives of those countries. The booty was hauled back to Spain on big ships called galleons. Those ships carried a lot of loose change, too. And most of the galleons came right through this very sea you're looking at."

"So the pirates started hanging around here so they could rob those ships," Jamal added. "It served those greedy Spaniards right!"

4

"Maybe it did," Ted said with a grin. "Anyway, there was a pirate ship called the *Laughing Moon* that sank near St. Lucia. Supposedly there was mucho treasure on board. That's the ship our underwater salvage team has been searching for."

"Have you found any sign of it yet?" Joe asked.

Ted shrugged. "Maybe we have, maybe we haven't. I've said too much already."

"Hey, that's not fair," Jamal said.

"A lot of things aren't fair," Dirk said with a playful wink.

"Catch you later, dudes," Ted said. Then he and Dirk strolled down the moonlit beach.

A few moments passed before Jamal said, "I read once that one third of all the gold ever mined is lying at the bottom of the world's seas and oceans. On sunken ships, of course."

"Maybe we should become underwater treasure hunters," Joe said. "I wonder if you can major in that in college."

"I bet those wrecks can be pretty tough to find," Frank said, always the practical one. "Chances are, playing the stock market is an easier way to get rich."

"Did somebody say rich?"

Frank turned and saw an elderly island woman standing right above him. Her skin was dark brown, like Jamal's, and her summery smock was the deep pink color of bougainvillea. "Hi, there," Frank said. "I didn't hear you coming."

"Hello, boys," the woman said with a deliciously thick island accent. "My name is Auntie Samantha. If you cross my palm with, oh, just a little bit of coin, I tell you a story."

"What sort of story?" Jamal asked.

"Any sort of story you want," the lady said, her smile revealing several missing teeth. "If it happened on this island, Auntie Samantha knows all about it. I know everything about this ol' heap of sand and trees on the water."

Frank pulled a few coins from the pocket of his cutoffs and handed them to Auntie Samantha. "How about a pirate story?"

"Ahhh, I know a whopping good pirate story," Auntie Samantha said. "Now get yourselves comfortable." She knelt on the sand, and the boys shifted to get in better positions to watch her. Auntie Samantha dramatically closed her eyes for a moment, as if summoning the story to her mind.

"You see, oh, about three hundred years ago," Auntie Samantha began, "there lived a young lady on this island by the name of Rebecca. She was from England, the daughter of a man who owned a banana plantation. There be many, many bananas on this island. Well, Rebecca was a very rich girl and a very merry girl, and she always wore a diamond necklace. But one sad day, tragedy crossed her path." Auntie Samantha spoke in a musical voice, her words mingling with the lapping of the waves and the rustling of the palms.

6

"One night," Auntie Samantha continued, "a beautiful night just like this, Rebecca was walking along the beach, not too far from here. Suddenly a band of grimy pirates sprang from the trees and rushed at Rebecca. They demanded the diamond necklace she wore. But because she dearly loved that necklace, Rebecca tried to fight the evil pirates away. And then, I am very sorry to report, the pirates murdered her."

"How?" Joe asked, his blue eyes flickering with interest.

"Some say they strangled her," Auntie Samantha told the boys. "Others say they slit her throat."

"Did they take the necklace?" Frank asked.

"Of course," Auntie Samantha said with a somber nod. "Then those grimy pirates, they returned to their ship and sailed away. But lo and behold, several hours later, by the light of the moon, they saw something moving on the waves in front of them. And do you know what that something was?"

"What?" Jamal asked.

"It was the ghost of Rebecca," Auntie Samantha said, her voice now hushed and low. "Rebecca's face was completely white, and she was walking on those waves just like she be walking on land. All the pirates rushed to the deck, and I'm sure some of them screamed with fright. Then those grimy pirates sailed away from these parts just as fast as their canvas sails would carry them."

"Was the ghost ever seen again?" Joe asked.

7

"I'm glad you ask that," the woman said. "Since that night, many a sailor has claimed to see the ghost of Rebecca. Last I heard of her being spotted was about, oh, I think five years ago. But I'm pretty sure ol' Rebecca is still out there. Still haunting the waves that roll toward this lovely little island, still looking for her beautiful diamond necklace,"

Auntie Samantha fell quiet, letting the rhythmic whisper of the waves put the finishing touch on the tale.

"Wow," Joe said after a moment. "That was a great story!"

"I'm glad you like it," Auntie Samantha said with a grateful bow. "If you boys ever want another story, you just come looking for Auntie Samantha. Most days you can find me inside the volcano." Auntie Samantha rose from the sand, brushed herself off, and glided down the beach as if she were being carried away by the trade wind.

"Did she say 'inside the volcano'?" Frank asked incredulously.

"There's a volcano on this island you can walk or drive through," Jamal explained. "It's called La Soufrière. It's the island's number-one tourist attraction."

"Let's put that on our list of vacation things to do," Joe said with enthusiasm. "Right after sleeping in and catching some rays."

For another few moments no one spoke. Gazing at the crescent moon, Frank let his imagination wander over the story he had just heard. As he pictured the ghost of Rebecca hovering on the sea, he now found the sound of the lapping waves to be somewhat ominous.

Then Frank saw something on the edge of the water that made his blood run cold. He closed his eyes, hoping the vision had been imaginary, but when he reopened his eyes, the frightening sight was still there.

"What's wrong?" Joe asked his brother.

"Look," Frank whispered, pointing.

Joe turned to look. The sight made his heart stop. Only several yards away, lying in the shallow water of the beach, was the limp body of a young woman.

2 Rescue

Frank, Joe, and Jamal sprang to their feet and ran over to the body. The young woman lay facedown in the white sand, the waves gently swishing her long chestnut hair up and down. She wore only shorts and a bathing-suit top.

After the boys pulled the young woman away from the water, Frank slapped her on the back a few times, right between the shoulder blades. Spurts of seawater came spraying from her mouth.

"Turn her over," Frank instructed, and Joe and Jamal turned the young woman onto her back. Her eyes were closed, and she appeared to be around twenty years old.

Frank placed an ear against her chest. "There's a heartbeat," he said. Then he tilted the young

10

woman's head back, pinched her nostrils, and put his mouth against her mouth in order to begin emergency resuscitation.

"She must have been swimming," Jamal said. "The tide probably saved her from drowning."

"Get the Jeep," Joe told Jamal. "Drive it down here if you can. Do you know where the hospital is?"

"I sure do," Jamal called, and darted away.

Joe watched as Frank blew repeatedly into the young woman's mouth. After several breaths Frank would pull back, then start again. Frank's effort continued for several tense minutes with no result, and Joe began to doubt the young woman would revive.

Finally Joe saw her chest expand. More seawater came dribbling from her mouth, and then her eyes popped open. "Good job, Frank," Joe said with relief.

"Thanks," Frank said, a bit winded.

With a groan, the young woman shut her eyes again. Joe noticed that she was tan and pretty.

A beige Jeep came roaring onto the beach, tires spewing white sand. Jamal braked the Jeep right near the young woman and leaped out. Frank and Jamal lifted her into the backseat of the Jeep. Then Joe got in back with her and covered her with a blanket while Jamal and Frank climbed into the front seats.

Most of the island was mountainous and covered

jungle-thick with trees and vegetation. Jamal had to pay close attention as he guided the Jeep down a steeply descending dirt road. Outside the beam of the Jeep's headlights was nothing but darkness.

The young woman was conscious but weak and groggy. Joe held a hand on her shoulder so she would not fall from the bumpy ride. She had been silent, her eyes mostly closed, but now Joe noticed she was trying to say something.

"Skeh . . ." the girl murmured in a hoarse voice.

"Shhh," Joe said. "Just relax right now. We're on the way to the hospital."

"Skeh . . ." she said again.

"What is it?" Joe asked, leaning close to her. "Do you need to tell me something?"

"Skeh . . ." she repeated.

"What's she saying?" Frank asked from up front.

"I don't know," Joe said. "It sounded like 'skeh.'"

"Maybe she's trying to say she's scared," Jamal said, shifting gears to accelerate the Jeep up a hill.

"Maybe," Joe said as the young woman shut her eyes once more.

Before long Jamal drove into the village of Soufrière, and within a few minutes he'd parked the Jeep in front of a two-story brick hospital. Joe and Jamal carried the young woman into the building, then set her on a chair inside the empty waiting room. Frank approached a nurse at a desk.

"What happened to her?" the nurse asked Frank.

12

"We don't know," Frank answered. "We found her lying on the beach. She had some water in her, but we got most of it out. I think she's in shock."

"Do you know who she is?" the nurse asked as she rolled a wheelchair over to the girl.

"Sorry," Frank said. "We have no idea."

"Okay, I'll take her right in to the doctor," the nurse said as Joe helped the young woman get into the wheelchair. Then the nurse wheeled her down the hallway.

Twenty minutes later a doctor wearing a white smock entered the waiting room. "Thanks to your efforts," the doctor said, approaching Jamal and the Hardys, "the patient is going to be all right. I pumped some more water out of her and, aside from that, she just needs a good night of rest. I wish I knew who she was, though. We'd like to notify her friends or family of her whereabouts, but we couldn't get any information from her."

"Could we see her briefly?" Frank asked. "Maybe we can get something out of her."

"I suppose," the doctor said with a nod. "She's in Room eleven. But stay only a few minutes, please."

"Right," Frank said, leading Joe and Jamal down the hallway. At Room 11 Frank rapped lightly at the door, then stepped into the room. Joe and Jamal followed. The room was dark, but enough light spilled in from the hallway for Frank to see the young woman lying on the tilted hospital bed.

13

As Frank approached, he could see her eyes were open. She was wearing a hospital gown and had an ID bracelet on her wrist. Her long chestnut hair was now dry and draped across the pillowcase. Though her face was friendly, there was a hint of fear in her pale blue eyes.

"How are you feeling?" Frank asked.

"Not too bad," the girl said, her voice still hoarse. "Are you the guys who brought me here?"

"That's right," Frank said. "I'm Frank Hardy. This is my brother, Joe, and our friend, Jamal Hawkins. What's your name?"

The young woman hesitated a long moment. "Uh . . . Chrissy," she said finally.

"Chrissy what?" Frank asked.

"I'd prefer we just leave it at Chrissy."

"Is there anyone we can notify about your being here?" Frank asked. "Some family or friends in the area?"

"No," Chrissy said quickly. "In fact, would you guys do me a big favor?"

"Sure," Frank said.

"Don't tell anyone you found me or brought me here," Chrissy said. "Please. Promise you won't say a word to anyone."

"Okay." Frank wondered what was up, but he said, "We promise."

"Do you remember what happened to you, Chrissy?" Jamal asked.

14

"No," Chrissy said, shaking her head. "I remember . . . some sort of struggle, then . . ."

"Who was struggling with you?" Jamal asked.

"I don't remember," Chrissy said, her brow wrinkling as if she were rummaging through her thoughts for some lost item. "Someone was trying to hurt me. . . . Suddenly I was in the water . . . and then . . . then I was swimming . . . and I, uh . . . just recall swimming and swimming a very long way until . . . I couldn't swim any farther."

"Chrissy?" Joe said, stepping toward the bed.

"Yes?" Chrissy said, turning to look at Joe.

"On the way here, you kept saying the word *skeh*," Joe said. "What does that mean?"

Chrissy looked at Joe a moment. She seemed to be trying to decide whether to reveal a piece of information. "I don't know," Chrissy said finally.

"All right," Frank said in a soothing voice. "Why don't you get some sleep and we'll come back to check on you in the morning? Good night, Chrissy."

"Good night," Chrissy whispered to the boys. "And listen—thank you."

Soon Jamal was steering the Jeep along a dark and snaking dirt road. Most of the island's roads were rough going and rarely straight or level.

"She's obviously scared of something," Jamal said, slowing down the Jeep for a curve. "Probably the person she was struggling with."

15

"That's why she wouldn't give us her last name," Joe said from the backseat. "That's also why she made us promise not to tell anyone we found her. And I bet she's hoarse from screaming. Something sinister is going on here."

"See, what did I tell you?" Jamal said. "It looks like the Hardy brothers have found themselves some trouble again."

"Not necessarily," Frank said, watching the darkened trees pass by. "Chrissy might just be mixed up from the trauma of nearly drowning. She genuinely didn't seem to remember most of what happened to her. Things might look a lot more reasonable when we see her in the morning."

"Let's hope so," Joe said as the Jeep hit a pothole.

Early the next morning Frank, Joe, and Jamal stepped out of the wooden bungalow where they were staying. It was a no-frills home with only a few rooms. The sun poured its warmth through the many types of trees clustered around the bungalow. The deep green leaves of the trees swayed with a slight breeze, and the branches were alive with the musical cries of birds. Even the air was sweet and fresh. The place was paradise.

"A great day for a vacation," Frank said.

"You can say that again," Jamal said. He showed the Hardys a skiff lying alongside the bungalow.

16

The old boat had obviously seen better days, and Joe could see where tar had been plastered over the cracks. An aged outboard motor was attached to the rear of the boat.

"It's not much to look at," Jamal told the Hardys, "but my uncle assures me it's seaworthy. In the front-room closet you'll find a box of boating supplies. Feel free to take out the skiff while I'm gone." Though Jamal's uncle was not staying on St. Lucia that month, Jamal had an appointment to fly one of her uncle's friends to a few neighboring islands for some business meetings.

"What time will you be back?" Frank asked.

"Our last stop is Martinique at four, and I'm leaving my passenger there," Jamal answered. "Why don't we meet here around, say, six? I'm pretty anxious to hear what you learn from Chrissy."

"We'll tell you everything," Frank said. "Have a safe flight." Jamal climbed into the Jeep, started the engine, and drove off.

"We can't visit Chrissy until nine," Joe said. "Why don't we wander down to the harbor and have a look around? You know, soak up a little local color."

"Excellent," Frank said.

They walked the short distance to the beach, then strolled along the sand for about a mile. A few tourists were already out sunbathing. By daylight

17

the water shimmered a gorgeous shade of turquoise, and Joe could see why people came from all over the world to visit the Caribbean beaches.

"Yes, sir," Joe said after a deep breath of sea air. "This is just what the doctor ordered. One carefree week on a tropical island."

"I'm glad you're enjoying yourself," Frank said, noticing the palm trees along the beach.

"Except," Joe said, "things won't be really carefree until we know Chrissy is okay."

Soon the Hardys reached the harbor. Numerous boats lingered on the water, some of them beginning to head out to sea. Joe admired a variety of yachts, powerboats, small and large sailing vessels, and fishing trawlers. He noted that many were expensive boats, obviously belonging to either tourists or the island's wealthier inhabitants.

Then Joe spotted a group of eight people standing by a dock, Ted and Dirk among them. Like the Hardys, most of the group wore shorts and T-shirts, and a few wore bathing suits. As the Hardys drew closer, Joe heard a heated exchange going on between two members of the group.

"Those two guys from last night are over there," Joe told Frank. "Maybe that's the crew that's looking for the *Laughing Moon*."

"They seem to be doing more fighting than laughing," Frank remarked.

The heated exchange turned into a yelling match. The two opponents were a thin weasel-like man and a big bear of a man. "I'm not saying that!" the thin man yelled.

"That's exactly what you're saying!" the bearlike guy yelled back.

Then the big guy took a threatening step toward the other man, who ran fearfully toward the Hardys. The bigger man dashed across the sand in pursuit and caught the man by the arm.

"Listen, Ziggy," the larger man shouted. "I've had about enough of you!"

"I wasn't accusing you of anything!" the other man protested. "Really, Lou, I wasn't!"

Lou cocked back a hairy arm, his fingers clenched in a big fist. He was about to turn Ziggy into hamburger.

3 The Scent of Treasure

As if he were back on the football field at Bayport High, Joe plowed into the large man's midsection. They both ended up sprawled on the sand, Joe on top.

"Hey, what's the big idea?" Lou roared. The next thing Joe knew, the bear of a man was on top of him, cocking back his fist again.

"I don't think so!" Frank said, catching Lou's hairy arm just in time.

By now the rest of the group had run over to the scuffle. "Come on, Lou," Dirk said as he pulled the guy off Joe. "It's no big deal. Chill out, man!"

Both Joe and Lou got up, panting heavily. Lou brushed sand out of his dark curly hair while Joe straightened his clothes and eyed the man. Lou appeared to be in his thirties and not bad looking as far as bears go. He wore a tattoo of an anchor on his powerful right bicep. Joe was glad to see Lou's anger was quickly subsiding.

"Sorry about that, guy," Lou said, offering a hand to Joe. "My temper gets the best of me sometimes. Thanks for stopping me. The name is Lou Brunelli."

"Hi, Lou," Joe said, shaking Brunelli's hand and introducing himself and his brother. Brunelli had a grip like a vise, and Joe was grateful he hadn't gotten the chance to see what Brunelli's fist felt like.

"I've got to admit," Brunelli said with admiration, "you've got some guts there, Joe." Brunelli then walked over to join some of the others in the group.

"We meet again," Ted said, nodding at Frank.

"What happened here?" Frank asked Ted.

"We're all on the underwater salvage crew," Ted explained. "It's been a real long search, and now and then we get a bit uptight. And we're especially uptight today."

"Why is that?" Frank asked.

"This gal on the crew, Chrissy, didn't come home last night, and she hasn't shown up this morning, either," Ted said. "We don't know if we should head out to sea to work or split up and look for her."

"Did you say her name was Chrissy?" Joe asked.

"That's right," Ted replied. "Chrissy Peters. Why, do you know of her?"

"Uh, no," Joe said, remembering his promise to Chrissy.

"I didn't think so," Ted said. "She's from the States, Virginia actually, and outside of the crew, I don't think she knows anyone on the island. She's a tough enough woman, so she should be all right. All the same, I'm worried."

Hearing another argument break out, Joe turned to look. Two other men from the group were exchanging heated words.

One was a tall man with dark wavy hair and a sharp nose, who Joe guessed was in his forties. He wore expensive clothing, sunglasses, and a jeweled ring that flashed on one finger. He was speaking with a French accent.

"Who's that?" Joe asked.

"That's Pierre Montclare," Ted said. "He owns a banana plantation on the island, and he's also the one financing our expedition. Apparently he was the last to see Chrissy. She was doing some book-keeping for him last night."

Frank and Joe exchanged a look.

"And who's the other guy?" Frank asked.

"Sandy Flask," Ted answered. "He's the captain of our expedition."

Flask looked as if he had spent his entire life at sea. His tanned face was textured with creases, his hair was a scraggly gray, and he wore a chain around his neck from which hung a gleaming gold coin. Though Sandy Flask was probably in his sixties, to Frank he had the air of someone who would live forever.

"No!" Montclare told Flask emphatically. "We cannot afford to miss a morning's work. The time is simply too valuable to me. *N'est-ce pas?*"

"But this woman could be in trouble," Flask said in a gravelly voice. "At the very least, we should send a few guys to check around town for her."

"The crew is small enough as it is," Montclare said.

Frank realized they were arguing about whether to look for Chrissy, but Chrissy apparently didn't want to be found. "Excuse me," Frank said, stepping up to Flask and Montclare. "Maybe my brother and I can help you out."

"Who are you?" Flask asked, eyeing Frank, then Joe.

"They're okay," Ted said, walking over. "I met them last night. In fact, they just stopped Brunelli from demolishing Ziggy."

Flask gave a gruff chuckle. "As you may have noticed," he said, "my crew is a little edgy these days. It always happens when men catch the scent of treasure. They change a bit, usually for the worse. All of a sudden, they turn greedy, suspicious, ornery."

"Have you found the pirate ship?" Joe asked, hoping Flask would be more forthcoming than Ted was the night before.

"Yeah, we found it a couple of weeks ago, out by Skeleton Reef," Flask said. "I told the crew not to tell anybody, but people come by in their boats, they see what's going on. As they say, the cat's out of the bag. I guess half the island knows we're hauling up treasure now."

"Congratulations," Frank said.

"Now, just how do you want to help out?" Flask said.

"My brother and I can check around town for Chrissy Peters," Frank said. "At the very least, we could stop by the police station and hospital. That way you guys can head right out to sea without missing any work time."

"Well, that's awfully neighborly of you," Flask said, looking at the Hardys with approval. "Here, I'll give you my ship-to-shore number so you can call me on my boat after you've done your checking. Tell the operator to charge it to me. I'm concerned about Chrissy, so call me right away." Flask wrote his number on a crumpled sheet of paper and handed it to Frank.

"We'll call you soon," Frank told him.

"Thanks a lot, mates," Flask said, tipping his captain's cap.

Moments later the Hardys watched the salvage crew head back toward the dock. "Good thinking,

Frank," Joe said once the crew was out of earshot. "This way we can ask Chrissy if she wants these guys to know where she is or not."

A little down from the docks, the Hardys saw a number of fishermen launching boats off the beach. The boats were mostly long wooden skiffs, none of which had motors, and the fishing equipment seemed to consist primarily of enormous nets. Mostly shirtless and barefooted, the fishermen went cheerfully about their work.

"What are you up to, mon?" Joe heard one fisherman say to another.

"Oh, not much at all, mon," the other fisherman replied with a casual wave.

"I noticed the fishermen by the docks had motorized boats," Joe said. "But I guess some of them prefer to do it the way it's been done since Columbus came passing through the neighborhood."

"Either that," Frank said, "or they can't afford the motors."

Looking back at the mainland, Frank admired the variety of vegetation on the island. Lush green trees and shrubs of all sizes and shapes stretched in every direction, some of the shrubbery showcasing brilliantly colored flowers. Then Frank noticed two towering cone-shaped mountains, one standing on either side of the bay as if they were guarding it against intruders. Both mountains were covered with a mossy green carpet.

"Jamal says those are called the Pitons," Joe

explained. "They were formed millions of years ago by volcanic eruptions. He says they're really something to see from out on the water."

"I bet they are," Frank said.

The brothers walked another mile along the beach until they came to the village of Soufrière. The center of town looked as if it hadn't changed much over the past hundred years. Most of the shops and offices were charming structures made of clapboard.

The people milling through the village were a mixture of tourists and islanders. Some of the island women were doing their morning shopping with wicker baskets on their heads. No one was dressed up, and Joe couldn't help but notice how relaxed and happy everyone seemed. There was a vacation air about the place, and that was just fine with Joe.

A battered bus roared wildly down a street, calypso music blaring from the radio. "How do you like that?" Frank said. "Musical buses."

"I like it, mon," Joe said with a big smile.

The Hardys stopped at an outdoor market and examined the fruit selection. Enticing baskets of bananas, mangoes, coconuts, pineapples, breadfruit, and melons sat on long tables. Frank and Joe each bought a mango for breakfast. "This is good," Joe observed as he sunk his teeth into the juicy orange fruit.

"It's almost nine," Frank said, looking at his watch. "Time to visit our friend Chrissy."

When the Hardys arrived at the hospital, there was a different nurse at the front desk. She told the brothers that Chrissy had been asleep when she last checked on her, an hour earlier. After obtaining visiting permission from the nurse, Frank and Joe walked down the hallway toward Chrissy's room.

Joe tapped lightly at the door of Room 11. Hearing no answer, they opened the door and peeked in. The morning sun shone brightly through the white curtains, which flapped in the breeze. Chrissy was nestled under the sheets of the bed.

"Chrissy?" Joe said softly. Chrissy did not stir or answer. "Chrissy?" Joe spoke a little louder.

When there was still no response, Joe walked over to the bed and touched Chrissy's shoulder. It was soft. Too soft. He was not touching a person. Joe peeled back the sheets and saw a collection of pillows laid out to imitate the shape of a human body.

The mysterious young woman named Chrissy Peters was gone.

4 The Destiny

"Chrissy's not here," Joe said, giving Frank an astonished look.

"Well, either someone took her or she escaped," Frank said, thoughtfully looking at the pillows on the hospital bed. "She probably left through the window, which explains why the nurse didn't see her leave."

"I say she escaped," Joe said, glancing at the gently flapping curtain. "I think somebody tried to kill her last night and she was afraid they might track her to the hospital. So she beat it as soon as she got her strength back."

"Hmm," Frank said, sitting on the bed. "I guess we've got two options now."

"Number one," Joe said, finishing Frank's train

of thought, "we stay out of this whole mess and enjoy our vacation. Number two, we get involved and try to figure out what's going on."

"If we stay out of this," Frank said, "Chrissy might remain in danger. And even if she manages to stay alive, the person who attempted to kill her will still be on the loose. Of course, we could go to the police, but then we would be breaking the promise we made to Chrissy about keeping all of this a secret."

"We're going to get involved, aren't we?" Joe said, sinking into a chair. "Goodbye, vacation. Hello, new case."

"I think it's for the best," Frank said quietly.

"So do I," Joe agreed. "It's funny, but I like Chrissy even though I barely know her. And the more I think about it, the creepier I feel, knowing someone is after her."

"Okay, little brother," Frank said. "Let's get to work."

Frank and Joe told the nurse of Chrissy's disappearance but revealed nothing else of what they knew about Chrissy. Then the Hardys headed outside into the sunshine.

"All right," Joe said as the brothers walked along the beach, heading back to the bungalow. "What do we know about Chrissy?"

"We know she's from Virginia, and we know she was part of Sandy Flask's crew," Frank replied.

"And Ted mentioned she didn't know anyone else on the island except for the crew members."

"Skeh!" Joe cried out. "Sandy Flask said he found the *Laughing Moon* on Skeleton Reef. Maybe Skeleton Reef is what Chrissy was trying to say."

"Maybe," Frank said as he passed a palm tree, "the person who tried to kill Chrissy was a member of the crew. They're the only ones around here Chrissy knows, and we've already seen that they're a scrappy gang."

"Let's call Flask and tell him we found no sign of Chrissy," Joe suggested. "Then let's ask if we can pay a little visit to Flask's boat. That will give us a chance to talk with the crew and sniff around for suspects."

"Sounds good," Frank said.

Back at the bungalow, Frank placed a ship-to-shore call to Sandy Flask at sea. Over the static of the connection, Frank told the captain he and Joe had visited the hospital and police station but hadn't seen or heard anything of Chrissy Peters. Then Frank asked if the Hardys could pay a visit to Flask's boat. Flask agreed and gave Frank instructions on how to find the vessel.

Thirty minutes later Frank and Joe were cruising on the Caribbean Sea in the beat-up skiff belonging to Jamal's uncle. Joe sat on the rear bench, operating the outboard, while Frank sat up front with a compass and a map. An expert at navigation, Frank was drawing intersecting lines on the map in order to find the precise location of Flask's boat. Both boys wore orange life jackets.

"Look behind you!" Joe called over the roar of the outboard.

Frank turned and caught a magnificent view of St. Lucia. From a distance the island was a curvaceous mass of green surrounded by a thin circle of beaches. On either side of the bay where the Hardys had been this morning, the cone-shaped Pitons rose majestically toward the clouds.

The view in the other direction wasn't bad, either. The Caribbean stretched toward the horizon, turquoise highlighted here and there with other shades of blue and green. The sun was beating down on the water, but a pleasant trade wind kept the air from being too hot. Not far away Frank saw a sailboat gliding gracefully in the breeze.

"Veer a few degrees starboard," Frank called, glancing at his compass. Joe swung the outboard engine a bit, and the skiff eased to the right.

After traveling four miles, the Hardys spotted a white speck in the distance. "That must be Flask's boat," Frank called out. As the skiff cut its way through the water, the white speck soon grew into the shape of an impressive vessel.

It turned out to be a cruiser with multitiered decks and a sizable cabin. A bare mast rose from the top deck, and Joe smiled when he saw the flag flying high atop the masthead. The flag was black

31

with a white skull and crossbones in the center—a Jolly Roger, the emblem of pirates.

"Ahoy there!" Flask called from the boat.

"Ahoy!" Frank called back.

"Tie up to port!" Flask shouted.

Joe maneuvered the skiff along the left side of Flask's boat. After tying a rope to the skiff, he threw the other end of the line to Flask, who lashed it to the side of his vessel. Then Frank and Joe climbed aboard the handsome white boat.

"Welcome aboard the *Destiny*," Flask said. "That's the name of this fine maiden. I don't usually allow outsiders on board, but you lads helped me out, and you look like you can handle yourselves."

"How's it going?" Joe asked, seeing the crew tending to their chores on the sun-drenched decks.

"Not great," Flask replied. "So far today the divers have been coming up empty-handed."

"Do you keep the *Destiny* anchored here?" Frank asked as he leaned on the gunwale, or railing, which he knew was pronounced "gunn'l." "I didn't see her anchored at the docks this morning."

"That's right," Flask answered. He pointed toward a weathered trawler tied alongside the opposite side of the boat. "We ride that claptrap fishing boat out here every day. The *Destiny* marks the dive site for us, and it also serves as a guard tower at night. See those two islanders?"

Flask pointed at two shirtless, dark-skinned men who were cleaning equipment on the top deck. One was big and muscular, Joe noticed, but the other was a giant.

"That's Isaac, and the big one's Ishmael," Flask explained. "They're cousins. They stay on the ship all night, one of them always awake. If anyone comes by with a mind to steal some of the *Laughing Moon* treasure out of the sea, Isaac and Ishmael shoo them away. I guarantee, no one messes with them."

"I can see why," Joe said.

Brunelli walked up to Flask and said, "We're getting ready to move into the new blasting position. Do you want to supervise?"

"Just follow my markings and call when you're set to drop anchor," Flask answered. "Frank, Joe, this is my first mate, Lou Brunelli."

"We've already met," Brunelli said, giving Joe a hard but friendly slap on the shoulder. Then Brunelli strode across the deck.

"What are you going to blast?" Frank asked.

With a half smile, Flask said, "You boys probably think we found this great old pirate ship down there, and all we have to do is crawl around the decks, opening chest after chest of treasure."

"It's not like that, is it?" Joe said.

"First of all," Flask said, "there is no ship anymore. The *Laughing Moon* was mostly made of wood, and all of it has long since rotted away or

33

been eaten by sea life. What's more, the treasure and artifacts have been scattered about by currents. We know the *Laughing Moon* went down right around this spot, but we have to search hard to find relics—especially since most of them are buried deep in the sand."

"So what are you going to blast?" Frank asked.

"See those things?" Flask said, pointing. Frank turned and saw two enormous, elbow-shaped aluminum tubes that hung over the rear of the boat.

"Those contraptions are called mailboxes," Flask explained. "They fasten right over the boat's propellers. We anchor the boat in a position that seems promising, then we lower the mailboxes, turn the engine on, and the mailboxes work with the propellers to blast two holes in the sand. A few divers look in the holes and others roam around, exploring elsewhere."

"All right, Peg, we're ready to move!" Brunelli called from the top deck. Just above the top deck was the main bridge, where the steering apparatus was located. At the helm a red-haired woman started the engine and guided the *Destiny* about twenty feet forward. "That's good," Brunelli shouted, and Peg shut down the engine.

"Prepare to drop anchor!" Flask called, surveying all points of the boat.

Frank and Joe moved to the rear, or stern, of the boat so they wouldn't block the captain's vision. Frank saw Montclare standing by one of the stern

34

anchor lines and Dirk standing by the other. He could see the weasel-like guy named Ziggy standing by the front, or bow, anchor line.

"Pierre, maybe you should let someone else handle that anchor," Flask called to Montclare. "You're not experienced enough."

"We're short a man today and I can manage it," Montclare called back. "Let's not waste time!"

Flask eyed Montclare mistrustfully, then pushed back his cap. "Drop the anchors!" the captain commanded. Montclare pulled a lever, and a motor began to whir.

Frank glanced at the anchor line, which was a coil of thick rope sitting on the deck a few feet away. He knew the rope fed through pulleys that lowered the line down with the anchor. But something was not right. The rope was feeding into the boat rather than out of it.

At the same time Frank and Montclare realized the lever had been pulled the wrong way. Montclare reversed the lever, and the rope swiftly uncoiled and shot through the pulleys onto the bottom of the sea.

Then something bit fiercely into Frank's ankle, and his feet flew out from under him.

35

5 The Laughing Moon

"Heeelp!" Frank yelled as he flew toward the stern. A section of anchor line had wrapped itself around his ankle and was yanking him straight for a pulley on the stern rail.

Joe got to his brother first. He grabbed hold of Frank and pulled, hoping to prevent his foot from being ripped to shreds in the pulley. But the force of the falling anchor was too powerful. Frank was slipping out of Joe's grasp.

"Shut it down!" Ted shouted as he also grabbed onto Frank. "Stop the anchor!"

Montclare shut down the motor. The rope stopped unwinding, but it was still tearing into Frank's leg as if it were the blade of a knife.

"Owww!" Frank cried out in pain.

Ted rushed to the anchor lever and reversed it. As the motor whirred again, rope began feeding back into the boat, causing enough slack in the rope for Frank to free his leg.

"Ahhh," Frank gasped as he sat up on the deck. He could see blood oozing through his sock.

"You okay, kid?" Flask said as he and several other crew members hurried over. "Ziggy, get the first-aid kit."

"I guess so," Frank said through gritted teeth.

"Montclare!" Flask boomed at the Frenchman.

"Listen!" Montclare yelled back. "Accidentally I hauled some line toward the boat first. This created some slack in the rope and that's what he got caught in. But the boy should have been watching."

"He's right," Frank said after a heavy breath. "I should have been paying more attention."

"All the same, Pierre," Flask said, "you shouldn't even be on the boat, let alone working one of the anchors. I don't know why I let you."

"I only did this today," Montclare argued, "because you lost a crew member! And if anyone should not be on the boat, it is these two boys."

Joe looked at the angry Frenchman. Maybe the anchor-line accident was Montclare's way of telling us he doesn't want us around, Joe thought.

"Okay, the show is over, folks!" Flask shouted to the crew. "Everyone back to work! Let's get that anchor down, then run the mailboxes." At once, all the crew members returned to their chores.

Ziggy handed Flask a first-aid box, and the captain knelt down to administer to Frank's leg. Frank sucked in his breath as Flask pulled down the bloody sock. There was an ugly gash running around Frank's ankle.

"Good thing you had socks on," Flask said as he poured hydrogen peroxide on the wound. "Otherwise it would have been a lot worse. The stars must be out of line today. First Chrissy is missing and now this."

Joe glanced at the two men in the stern who were tilting the mailboxes into the water. He'd learned from Flask that the one with a beard was Vines and the one with a mustache was Wilson. Joe was keeping careful track of everyone on the *Destiny*. One of them could very well be the person after Chrissy Peters.

The engine was turned on and the aluminum mailboxes rattled loud as lawn mowers. "The boxes are blasting now," Flask told the Hardys as he cut a bandage with scissors.

"So tell me, Mr. Flask," Frank said, wanting to get his mind off his injured leg. "How did you manage to find the *Laughing Moon*?"

"Well," Flask began, "the *Laughing Moon* was a famous pirate ship in its time, and its captain, Black Dan Cavendish, was pretty famous, too. Supposedly he and his band captured as much Spanish treasure as any of the buccaneers. Then, in the year 1712, the *Laughing Moon* disappeared. Some figured

Black Dan sailed the ship to Africa, while others figured the vessel fell victim to bad weather."

"Has anyone else besides you looked for the *Laughing Moon?*" Joe asked.

"Oh, lots of folks," Flask said with pride. "But none of them ever saw a trace of it." Flask wrapped the bandage around Frank's ankle, and continued, "I was determined to find it. First, I went to Spain. They've got a big library in Seville where they keep all the logs and records from the old Spanish vessels. Boys, I spent an entire year in that library, poring over scribbled ink on yellowed parchment. Fortunately, I'm pretty good with Spanish."

"Sounds like school," Joe said.

"I found every reference I could to the *Laughing Moon,*" Flask continued. "And then I studied old weather reports of every location where the *Laughing Moon* was seen and every location where it might have been. Just when I was about to ruin my eyes, I figured things out. I had a good notion that in July of 1712, a storm forced the *Laughing Moon* onto Skeleton Reef. There, I figured, the rough coral of the reef ruptured the hull, and the boat sank."

"This reef must be especially treacherous to ships," Frank said.

"That's why they call it *Skeleton* Reef," Flask said, chuckling as he taped Frank's bandage.

Joe heard the engine shut down and the mailboxes stop rattling. Four crew members in diving gear jumped off a ledge at the boat's stern. "So you went to Skeleton Reef and looked around for the *Laughing Moon*," Joe said, turning back to Flask.

"It wasn't that simple," Flask said. "It took me another solid year to persuade the St. Lucia government to grant me the rights for the search and then to find someone to finance my work. Finally I made those two things happen and was ready to go."

"And then you found the ship," Joe said.

"Then I started *looking*," Flask said, jabbing Joe with his finger. "For two years my crew and I sailed around these waters dragging a magnetometer behind us."

"Oh, one of those iron-detecting devices?" Frank said.

"Right," Flask said. "If the mag readout showed a large quantity of iron in the water, we would anchor the boat and dive down to check things out. We found the remains of some old heap of a boat more than once, and we found some even more worthless things, like a discarded washing machine. We also had to keep careful records of where we had been so we wouldn't cover the same area twice."

"Wow," Joe said, wiping sweat from his face, "that sounds like a tremendous amount of work."

"Kid, let me tell you something," Flask said, squinting from the sun. "Treasure hunting isn't a profession, it's an affliction. Finding a ship in the sea is like finding a needle in a haystack—only harder. You can spend your entire life searching for something you'll never even get close to."

"But in this case, you succeeded," Frank said.

"Finally, two weeks ago," Flask said, "the mag led us to some iron cannons. Then nearby we found some Spanish coins dated 1710 and 1711. When we found some jewelry, I consulted my records of what was known to have been stolen by Black Dan and his men. Sure enough, the stuff checked out, and I knew I had found remnants from the *Laughing Moon.* Yes, sir, it was the sweetest day of my crazy life."

Flask talked some more about the *Laughing Moon*, then regaled the Hardys with colorful stories from other salvage expeditions he had led. Frank found it interesting that Flask was having trouble paying his monthly rent even though he was a professional treasure hunter. After twenty minutes the sight of the divers breaking through the water interrupted Flask's storytelling.

Everyone gathered around as the four divers climbed onto the deck. "We got some goodies this time!" Vines called, pulling off his face mask. Then the divers began unloading the net bags they carried.

Most of the objects were so encrusted with a grayish substance that it was impossible to tell what they were. Then some blackened coins tumbled to

incredibly valuable relics, maybe millions of dollars' worth, but meanwhile the crew members are living at poverty level."

"What a bummer," Joe said.

"It's mucho frustrating," Brunelli said, clenching and unclenching his big fist. "I think that's why I lost my cool this morning. And, again, I'm sorry about that."

As Joe watched four more crew members in diving gear jump off the boat, Flask approached. "Do you boys dive?" the captain asked the Hardys.

"We love to," Joe said eagerly. "And we're both certified. Do you have some extra gear?"

"Frank is on the injured list," Flask replied, "but, Joe, if you want to have a look at the reef, get Ted to suit you up."

"Thanks!" Joe sprang to his feet. Soon he was decked out in scuba gear: mask, fins, weight belt, oxygen tank, and a diver's watch. He wore his cutoffs and the top of a rubber wet suit. "You've got thirty minutes of air," Ted said as he adjusted Joe's tank. "Don't go far, and keep a close eye on your watch."

"I understand," Joe said, pulling his mask down and making sure the fit was snug.

"That's funny," Ted said, glancing at the compressor used to fill the divers' tanks.

"What?" Joe asked.

"The oxygen level is lower than it should be," Ted said, studying a dial. "I bet Isaac and Ishmael

44

are diving off the boat at night. They're not supposed to, but it's no big deal. Okay, have a great swim, Joe."

"I will," Joe said. He walked to the stern, his fins slapping on the deck. Putting in his mouthpiece, he sucked a breath of compressed air. Feels right, he thought as he pushed a button to activate his diver's watch. Then Joe leaped off the stern ledge, his legs spread for distance, and hit the water with a forceful splash.

As the weight of his belt pulled him downward, Joe glanced at the underwater world around him. The water was as clear as glass. Joe glimpsed the bright colors of coral at some distance below and nearby saw the white hull of the *Destiny*.

Keep breathing, Joe reminded himself.

Under the rear of the hull, he saw a flurry of sand drifting upward, which he knew was caused by the mailboxes. As he drifted farther down, Joe could vaguely make out three of the *Destiny*'s divers working near the sea floor.

I'll check them out later, Joe thought. First, a brief survey of the reef. He turned himself horizontal and, using a flutter kick, propelled his body toward the corals on the floor.

Joe knew coral reefs were areas where large shelves of coral grew not far from the water's surface. Because the coral was as hard as a rock and as sharp as a stiletto, it could be quite dangerous to ships—and divers.

Soon Joe was on top of Skeleton Reef. Up close the coral was spectacular. It blossomed out of the sea floor and spread branches like a never-ending tree. The colors were fluorescent—green, pink, orange, and yellow. As he swam, he was careful not to scrape against the coral.

Joe glimpsed a school of fish swimming through the coral branches. There were hundreds of them, colored an almost transparent purple. With all the colors wavering in the water, he felt as if he were looking inside a gigantic kaleidoscope.

Then Joe glimpsed a much larger fish swimming toward the coral. No, Joe realized, it seems to be swimming toward me! He drew a sharp breath from his mouthpiece.

Joe knew a shark when he saw one.

6 Out of the Sand

Joe's first impulse was to swim away as fast as possible, but he knew that would be the wrong thing to do. If it wanted to, the shark could catch him easily. And furthermore, the movement would only entice the shark. Joe knew the best thing to do was remain calm and stay still. He inhaled a shot of compressed air, reminding himself to continue breathing.

The shark glided closer, moving effortlessly through the crystalline water. The creature was long, sleek, and bluish gray. There was an angled fin on each side of the shark's body and another angled fin on top of the back. Joe knew the fins helped keep the shark buoyant in a manner similar to the wings of an airplane.

Joe also knew sharks were not nearly as dangerous as their reputation—at least not to humans. The fact was, sharks usually had little interest in human flesh.

As the shark glided closer, Joe noticed the yellowish eyes set far back in the head. Then he glimpsed dozens of razor-sharp teeth set inside the shark's enormous mouth.

Keep breathing! Joe told himself.

The shark began swimming in a slow circle around Joe, obviously studying him. Joe knew the shark was probably relying on vibrations rather than sight to sense what sort of a creature he was. However it did it, the shark soon decided he was not a tempting enough snack and began swimming away.

As Joe let out a breath of relief, he saw a parade of tiny bubbles float up from his mouthpiece. Never underestimate how perilous the sea can be, Joe told himself. Even the gorgeous corals of the reef around him were potentially deadly.

This reminded Joe to check his watch. Seven minutes had elapsed on his dive. Okay, he thought, I should pay a visit to the *Destiny* divers. Who knows? I might even pick up some sort of clue I wouldn't have discovered on deck.

Joe propelled himself toward the spot where he knew the divers were working. It was some distance away from the coral and deeper down. Below him,

Joe saw Ziggy swimming here and there, running his hand along the sea floor.

Soon Joe was swimming through clouds of swirling sand. Looking down, he saw two craters, each about four feet deep, which had been created in the sea floor by the mailbox blasts.

Through the sandy water, Joe saw Dirk and Wilson digging inside one of the craters with gardening spades. The divers had knives strapped to their legs and net bags attached to their wrists.

After hovering above the crater a few minutes, Joe saw Dirk pull an object out of the sand. While Dirk and Wilson examined the object with great interest, Joe swam closer for a better look. Though the object was partially covered with encrustation, he could see it was a leather shoe. Almost three hundred years ago, the shoe had been on the foot of a pirate!

As Dirk placed the shoe in his net bag, Joe turned around to get a look inside the other crater. The red-haired young woman named Peg was working alone in it. Through the swirling sand, Joe saw her chipping at the crater wall with her spade. Working with a great deal of determination, she seemed to know something was there. With each chip, more sand drifted upward.

A host of tiny objects began floating up in the midst of the sand. Joe felt his heartbeat increase when he saw what the objects were—dozens of glittering gold coins. The coins glinted as they caught the sunlight filtering down from the surface. It was a magical sight.

Joe continued hovering above the crater, but Peg was too busy to notice him. She began grabbing at the coins and placing some of them in her bag. When the other coins settled, she began scooping them off the bottom of the crater.

Next Joe saw something very interesting. Peg partly unzipped the top of her wet suit, placed several handfuls of coins inside it, then rezipped.

Peg did some more chipping at the crater wall, then pulled out a number of encrusted objects. Some of the objects went in her bag, but a few of the smaller ones went into her wet suit.

Finally Peg checked her watch. Then she pushed out of the crater and began swimming upward. Joe quickly swam away. From a distance he watched Peg kick her way up through the sandy water for a moment. Glancing at his diver's watch, Joe saw he had been down twenty-two minutes. Time to go. He followed Peg upward.

Joe broke through the surface of the water and saw Peg climbing the ladder on the side of the *Destiny*. Joe swam to the boat, climbed the ladder, and stepped onto the boat himself.

As Joe pulled off his mask and spit out his mouthpiece, Peg set her net bag on the deck. Teisenbach was there, already going through the items brought up by Dirk and Wilson.

"How was it?" Frank asked, approaching Joe.

"See that redhead?"

"You mean Peg," Frank said, looking at her.

"I saw her hide some coins and artifacts inside her wet suit," Joe said. "She's not handing them over to the archaeologist, either. I think she's planning to steal them. I'm wondering if this might have something to do with the Chrissy situation. As you know, where there's one crime, there's often another."

As Peg moved away from Teisenbach, Frank and Joe both watched her. She removed all her diving gear but kept on the top of her wet suit. Next she moved to the bow and picked up a duffel bag. Then she carried the duffel bag down the steps leading into the cabin.

"I'm going to follow her," Frank told Joe.

Frank waited a moment before walking toward the cabin area. When he stepped through the door, he found himself in a closed-in corridor. A door to the right was marked Rest Room, a door to the left was marked Storage, and beyond the corridor were two rooms.

Hearing running water in the rest room, Frank realized Peg was inside. Frank waited by the door.

After returning his diving gear, Joe spotted Montclare sitting near the bow. He was reading a paperback book, obviously uninterested in the seafaring activity around him. Joe considered Montclare to be near the top of the suspect list. He'd been the last to see Chrissy, and he'd made light of mangling Frank's leg, as well.

"Hi," Joe said, approaching Montclare.

"*Bonjour*," Montclare said, only briefly glancing up from his book. A bottle of sunscreen lay beside him.

"Do you normally spend time on salvaging ships?" Joe asked.

"No," Montclare said, eyes on his book.

"I see," Joe replied. "Have you, uh, ever financed an expedition like this before?"

"No," Montclare said into the book again.

"What's your normal line of work?" Joe asked.

"Bananas," Montclare muttered.

"Ah, bananas," Joe said, crouching down. "I've never met anyone in the banana business before. I like bananas, though. I'm especially fond of banana splits. Have you ever had one of those? It's a combination of ice cream, sliced bananas, and—"

"Listen," Montclare said, slamming down his book. "I don't know why you are on this boat, but I don't want you coming back. You and your brother are not covered by my insurance plan. If you were to be seriously injured, you could sue me. Furthermore, I don't like to be interrogated like I am some sort of criminal! Do you understand? Good. *Adieu.*" Montclare picked up his book and resumed reading.

"*Adieu* to you, too," Joe muttered and walked away.

Below deck, Frank was still waiting outside the rest room.

Finally Peg came out. "Oh, hello," she said in surprise. "I'm sorry if I kept you waiting."

"It's okay," Frank said with a friendly smile. "I just got here. I'm Frank Hardy, by the way."

"Good to meet you," Peg said, shaking Frank's hand. "My name is Peg Riley."

Frank guessed she was in her twenties. Her freckled face was attractive, but she also had an air of toughness. Her eyes were an intense shade of green, and she spoke with a strange yet appealing accent.

"Where are you from, Peg?" Frank asked.

"Ireland," Peg answered.

"Wow," Frank said, leaning against the wall. "How did you wind up in the Caribbean?"

"Well, like most of the folks in the treasure-hunting business," Peg said in her lilting accent, "I guess I'm a bit of a drifter. None of us is the type to stay in one place and hold down a regular job. You might call us restless spirits."

"Maybe that's what happened to that woman who didn't show up today," Frank said, as if just making conversation. "What was her name?"

"You mean Chrissy?" Peg asked.

"Yes," Frank said. "Maybe Chrissy just felt the need to drift to somewhere else."

"Perhaps," Peg replied. "But she didn't take any of her things with her."

"How do you know?" Frank asked.

"The two of us share a little bungalow near Soufrière," Peg explained. "Actually it's more like a shack. Aside from being drifters, most of us are also as poor as church mice."

"As long as you're not rats," Frank said with a laugh. Peg smiled tightly, obviously not amused by the joke.

"Are you worried about Chrissy?" Frank asked.

"A bit," Peg said. "But aside from being drifters, most of us are pretty savvy, too. I imagine Chrissy can take care of herself."

"And it's not like anyone was out to get her, is it?" Frank said in a casual manner.

"What are you, a detective?" Peg asked, her green eyes piercing Frank.

"No, just a curious kid," Frank said, shrugging.

Peg seemed to believe him. "No one would be out to get Chrissy," she told Frank. "She's a nice girl from the States. Shy even. Most of us have made some friends on the island, but Chrissy kept mostly to herself. And now, Frank, if you'll excuse me, I have work to do upstairs. A pleasure to meet you."

Peg gave Frank a nod, then left the cabin. If she's a liar, he thought, she's a fairly good one.

Frank decided to stay in the cabin area and look

around. He poked his head inside one of the rooms. It was a galley containing a refrigerator, stove, pantry, and cooking supplies. He stepped into the other room, which contained two narrow beds and a desk. Some clothes were lying on the floor, and he figured they belonged to Isaac and Ishmael, the cousins who guarded the dive site.

Frank glanced at some papers on the desk. One of the sheets listed the names, current addresses, and phone numbers of the *Destiny* crew. The paper also contained information on everybody's next-of-kin, which he realized was necessary in case anybody was seriously hurt or killed during work. After some rummaging, Frank found another copy of the list. He folded it and put it in the back pocket of his cutoffs.

While looking at a large map of the reef area, he became aware of another person's presence. Frank spun around and saw Isaac watching him from the doorway.

"Hello, mon," Isaac said in a deep voice.

"Hi," Frank replied. "I was just, uh . . . just having a little look around."

Isaac walked over to a corner of the room and picked up a rifle Frank hadn't seen. Opening a drawer in the desk, Isaac pulled out a box of bullets. He loaded several bullets into the rifle chamber.

"Just having a look around?" Isaac said as he closed the chamber with a loud click.

"That's right," Frank said, wondering what the gun was for. "It's an awfully nice boat you folks have here."

Isaac lifted the rifle to eye level and aimed it at Frank.

Frank swallowed. Was this his last precious moment on earth?

7 Scavengers

"What's the matter?" Isaac asked, keeping the rifle in Frank's face. "Am I scaring you?"

"As a matter of fact, you are," Frank answered as calmly as possible. "If you're planning to shoot me, perhaps you could give me some indication why."

A smile spread across Isaac's face. "Aw, I'm just having some fun with you, mon," Isaac said, lowering the rifle. "This rifle isn't for you. It's for somebody else."

Isaac walked out of the room and out of the cabin area. Curious about who the rifle was intended for, Frank followed Isaac up to the deck.

Flask, Joe, Ishmael, and several other crew members were standing by the gunwale on the port side of the boat. Isaac approached the gunwale with his rifle, and Frank joined the group.

Shielding his eyes from the sun, Frank saw a boat cutting through the water straight for the *Destiny*. It was a fiberglass powerboat, and Frank could hear gales of laughter over the engine's roar. "Don't shoot unless you have to," Flask told Isaac, keeping his eyes on the approaching boat.

"No, skipper, I won't," Isaac replied.

"Who is that?" Frank asked Flask.

"That's Rob and Davy," Flask said gruffly. "They're a couple of blokes from Australia. Scavengers is what they are."

"How do you mean?" Frank asked.

"Whenever some guy like me locates a sizable treasure somewhere," Flask explained, "Rob and Davy always manage to find out about it. I don't care if it's the Caribbean or the Mediterranean or the Amazon, they show up."

"What do they do?" Joe asked.

"They try to steal the treasure," Flask said after a spit in the water. "Any way they can. They might sneak underwater at night, or they might fight you off with guns in broad daylight. They even blew a guy's boat up once. They're dirty dogs, both of them. Crazy, too. Real crazy."

Moments later the powerboat stopped beside the *Destiny*, engine idling. Joe appraised the two men standing in the boat. One was short with a crooked nose, the other tall with a nasty scar on his cheek.

Both men wore baseball caps over their longish hair and neither had shaved for several days. Though they seemed to be in their forties, the men were giggling like a pair of devious schoolboys.

"Rob's the squirt," Flask told the Hardys. "Davy's the taller one."

"Ahoy there, Captain Flask!" Rob called out. "I understand you've found some nice pirate treasure out here."

"Some *very* nice treasure!" Davy added. The men spoke with Australian accents, which sounded like a rougher version of an English accent.

"That's right," Flask called back. "I spent four years looking for it, and I've got no intention of sharing a single ingot with the likes of you two!"

"You don't have to be so hostile," Davy called.

"No, we were just thinking, Davy and me," Rob called, "that maybe you could use a few extra hands."

"We'll do whatever you say, Captain," Davy said. "All you have to do is give us a teeny-weeny, itsy-bitsy piece of the pie!" At that, Rob and Davy burst into raucous laughter.

"Sorry," Flask barked. "I've got all the help I need. Besides, I don't like scum on my decks."

"I see," Rob called, rubbing his stubbly chin. "Well, what if something unfortunate were to happen to a couple of your crew members? Would you be needing some additional help then?"

"If you touch anybody on my crew," Flask said,

"I'll make sure you two never take a breath of anything but seawater again. Got it? Now scram! I have been granted exclusive rights to this site by the St. Lucia government."

"Aw, Captain," Davy called out, "there's no need to be using harsh words. We're all friends here."

"I said scram!" Flask thundered.

"It's a free sea!" Rob yelled. "We'll scram when we've got a mind to scram!"

"Isaac," Flask said quietly.

Isaac lifted his rifle to eye level. Then he pulled the trigger, and a shot resounded in the open air. Isaac fired again. Joe could see Isaac was aiming wide of the Australians, trying only to scare them.

"On second thought," Rob called out, "maybe we'd better scram now. Don't worry though, Captain, you haven't heard the last of us!"

"Oh, no!" Davy added. "Not by a long shot."

The two Australians howled with laughter as they turned their boat around and zoomed away.

"Good work, Isaac," Flask said. "From now on, I want you and Ishmael to be extra careful. Crazy as they are, those guys are smart and dangerous—like a pair of hyenas."

"Fear not, Skipper," Isaac said. "Isaac and Ishmael can handle those two just fine." Ishmael gave one nod, then the two cousins headed back to their post on the top deck.

"Isaac and Ishmael," Flask told the Hardys,

"they're not afraid of anything. Well, no, maybe there's one thing they're afraid of."

"What's that?" Frank said, watching Rob and Davy's boat disappear in the sun's glare.

"There's a ghost that supposedly haunts the waters around here," Flask said.

"Rebecca," Joe said.

"Yeah, I think that's her name," Flask said, fingering the gold coin around his neck. "One night Isaac and Ishmael thought they saw the ghost, and it near scared them to death. I don't believe in ghosts myself, but some of these island folk are pretty superstitious."

Using this as a cue, Flask began telling the Hardys a few tales of his travels around the many Caribbean islands. He seemed to have no shortage of stories, but after half an hour he left to consult with Brunelli over some nautical matter.

"What did you find out about the redhead?" Joe asked, once the Hardys were alone.

The sun was beating down hard on the deck, and Frank wiped sweat from his forehead. "Her full name is Peg Riley," he said. "I think she transferred the stolen goods to her duffel bag. It also turns out she's Chrissy's roommate."

"Interesting," Joe said, brushing back his blond hair. "Maybe she's been bringing her stolen goods home, and Chrissy found them. That would give Peg a reason to attack Chrissy."

"She didn't seem all that worried about Chrissy, either," Frank added.

"I had a chat with Pierre Montclare," Joe said.

"What did he have to say?" Frank asked.

"Not much," Joe replied. "He said he's in the banana business and he didn't want us on the boat because we're not covered by his insurance policy. I didn't get to ask anything about Chrissy. He seemed to be in an awfully foul mood."

"Something occurred to me while you were diving," Frank told Joe. "The person who tried to kill Chrissy might believe she died in the water last night. What I'm saying is, we might look for signs of guilt in the people we speak to today. For example, that could explain why Montclare was in such a bad mood."

"I'll keep that in mind," Joe said. "Then again, not all criminals show any sign of guilt."

"That's true," Frank said.

Frank saw Brunelli approaching. He was cleaning his fingernails with some object, and Frank realized it was the type of spear used with a speargun. "You boys seem awfully interested in this expedition," Brunelli said, leaning on the gunwale.

"It's interesting stuff," Frank said.

"I guess it is," Brunelli said, glancing from Frank to Joe. "Especially if you're not here every day. It's mostly a lot of hard work. Sweating on this deck, hauling equipment, groping through the sand."

"Look at this, boys," Flask said as he approached

the Hardys. He was holding a clear plastic bag filled with water, and inside the bag was the leather shoe Dirk had brought up.

"What's the water for?" Frank asked.

"We keep all the relics soaking in seawater," Flask explained. "It keeps them from breaking apart before they're properly treated."

Frank wondered if Peg had filled bags with water to keep her stolen relics intact. It was possible she had done just that in the rest room, he figured, maybe even sprinkling salt in the bags to simulate seawater.

"You know something, boys," Flask said, eyeing the shoe fondly, "this thing is more valuable to me than anything we've found so far. You can keep all the silver, gold, and jewels. I'll take this dilapidated old scrap of footwear."

Brunelli was still cleaning his fingernails with the spear. "Sandy, I wish I *could* keep all the gold and silver," he said with a bitter laugh. "But, unfortunately, I can't." Then Brunelli tapped the spear against Frank's shoulder and walked away.

"Why is the shoe so valuable to you?" Joe asked.

"Because it's like a fragment of the pirate past coming back to life," Flask said with excitement. "I look at this shoe and can almost see the man who wore it. His skin tanned and leathery from the sun. His fingers gnarled from working the ropes. His body scarred from countless brawls and battles. I imagine his name was Bart."

"You're fascinated by pirates, aren't you, sir?" Frank asked, amused by Flask's enthusiasm.

"Yes, indeed, I am," Flask admitted. "Pirates, not money, are the reason I spent so much time looking for the *Laughing Moon*. And I feel a special kinship with its captain, Black Dan Cavendish."

"What was he like?" Frank asked.

"A fearsome fellow but also quite intelligent," Flask said as if he knew the man personally. "He was an officer in the British Navy before he decided to join the piratical trade. During those four long years I spent looking for this ship, I got pretty frustrated from time to time. But every once in a while, in the darkest hours of night, I could almost hear Black Dan talking to me."

"What would he say?" Joe asked, intrigued.

"Black Dan," Flask said, almost whispering, "he would tell me, 'Keep looking, Sandy, ol' boy. Keep looking. I want you to be the one to find the *Laughing Moon*, and I know you will. Yes, mate, I know you will.'"

"I thought you didn't believe in ghosts," Frank said, raising an eyebrow at Flask.

"Well, maybe I do just a bit," the captain confessed.

Frank and Joe spent another two hours on the *Destiny*, during which time they managed to speak with every person on board. The cast consisted of Flask, Montclare, Brunelli, Peg, Ted, Dirk, Ziggy, Vines, Wilson, Isaac, Ishmael, and Teisenbach, the archaeologist. Aside from Montclare and Peg, the Hardys found no one especially suspicious. Finally the Hardys thanked Captain Flask for his hospitality and climbed down into their humble wooden skiff.

After the skiff was unlashed, Joe yanked the cord, and the outboard motor roared to life. The Hardys began cruising homeward through the turquoise water. Some dark clouds were drifting into the sky, but they didn't seem threatening.

Ten minutes later, however, Frank heard a sound that bothered him more than any rumble of thunder ever had. It was the sound of raucous laughter mixed with a powerboat's engine.

Rob and Davy were speeding toward the Hardys, leaving a trail of white foam in their wake. "Are they coming after us?" Frank asked from the bow.

"I think so," Joe said, looking worried.

"Ahoy there!" Rob called, waving his arms.

"Keep going," Frank said. "We can't outrun them, but we can ignore them."

"Ahoy!" Rob shouted again as the powerboat closed in fast on the Hardy's skiff.

Davy picked up a brown bottle. The next moment he seemed to be holding something to the bottle's neck. "What is he . . ." Joe began.

Davy heaved the bottle through the air. Several yards away from the Hardys, the bottle exploded, spraying glass in all directions.

Rob and Davy howled with crazy laughter.

"That was a bomb!" Joe exclaimed.

"I know, and it looks like they've got more," Frank said, seeing the scavengers each pick up a new bottle.

Still guffawing, Rob and Davy were lighting their bottle bombs. "What are we going to do?" Joe cried out. "If one of those bombs hits us, it could sink our boat!"

Rob and Davy heaved their bombs at the Hardys' skiff. Horrified, Frank knew he and his brother were running out of luck.

8 Blood in the Water

"Swing!" Frank called.

Joe jerked the outboard handle, and the boat veered to starboard. The bombs exploded to port, showering Frank and Joe with glass fragments.

"Are you okay?" Frank called to his brother.

"Fine," Joe shouted back.

The powerboat pulled up alongside the skiff, and Rob cut back the engine to keep pace with the Hardys. Frank glimpsed a basket filled with the brown bottle bombs inside the boat. He also noticed Rob had a pistol tucked into his pants.

"Where are you boys running off to?" Rob called. "The party is just starting!"

"Yeah, right," Joe said sarcastically. "Why don't you crash somebody else's party."

Frank wished they could speed away, but he knew they didn't have enough horsepower to out-race Rob and Davy's boat. He scanned the sea, hoping there was a vessel nearby to help out in case of trouble. There was nothing around but miles of water.

"How do you like serving on Captain Kidd's crew?" Rob asked, keeping the powerboat abreast of the skiff. "Oh, I mean, Captain Flask."

"We're not members of the crew," Frank replied. "We were just visiting for the day. What's it to you?"

"Are you sure you're not members of the crew?" Davy asked. "You looked like crew members."

"Because if you *were* members of the crew," Rob said with a wicked leer, "we might want to make you go away. That way we'd get to be members of the crew."

"Dream on," Joe muttered.

"Look, we don't work for Flask," Frank added.

"You know what I think, Davy?" Rob said, lifting a bomb from the basket.

"What's that, Robby boy?" Davy asked, also grabbing a bomb.

"I think they're lying," Rob said with a sneer.

"So do I," Davy said with a chuckle.

"Why don't we teach them a lesson?"

"Indeed, I think they need it!"

Frank watched in horror as Rob and Davy flicked lighters, then lit the rope fuses sticking out from the bottles. Joe turned the skiff away, but Frank knew there was nowhere to run. Rob and Davy held their lit bombs a few seconds so they would explode almost immediately after being thrown.

"Swing!" Frank yelled as Rob and Davy tossed the bombs. Joe swung the skiff to port, but both bombs landed inside the skiff, right by his feet. Joe reached for the bombs, but Frank could see the flames on the fuses were almost at the glass.

"Get away from them!" Frank shouted.

Joe scurried toward the front of the skiff just as the bombs exploded. The noise made his ears ring.

"Fare thee well!" Rob shouted.

"Happy Fourth of July!" Davy bellowed.

Cackling with crazy laughter, Rob and Davy sped away from the skiff, foam spewing in their wake. The skiff rocked roughly on the waves created by the powerboat.

Except for a few minor glass cuts, the Hardys were uninjured by the bombs—but the same was not true of the skiff. "We're in trouble," Frank said. He pointed to two long cracks on the skiff's floor. Water was seeping into the boat.

"Should we start bailing?" Joe asked.

"We'll never be able to keep up with the flow of water," Frank said, opening a wooden supply box the boys had brought from the bungalow. He pulled out a flare gun and two flares.

As the water rose to his ankles, Frank loaded a flare into the small pistol. "Here goes," he said, aiming the pistol into the air. He pulled the trigger, the cylinder whistled up to the sky, and soon the cylinder was trailing a stream of red smoke.

"Why isn't anyone around?" Joe asked, still not seeing a single vessel on the horizon.

"Maybe because it's so cloudy," Frank said, noticing more dark clouds drifting overhead.

The Hardys remained in the skiff another few minutes, hoping a vessel would come after someone spotted the red distress signal. Each tense and silent moment seemed to stretch into hours. When the stern began angling into the sea, Frank shot the second and final flare.

"After you," Frank said to his brother in a grim tone.

Joe jumped into the water, Frank right after him. As they watched the skiff sink lower, the Hardys floated in the warm water, made buoyant by the foam in their life jackets. Having no better choices, they began swimming in the direction of St. Lucia.

After fifteen minutes the Hardys stopped to rest, floating on their backs. Frank scanned the water in every direction, seeing only a lone seagull soaring by. Then Frank saw a most unwelcome sight.

"Don't panic," Frank told Joe, "but I see a few sharks headed our way."

Joe turned. In the distance he saw the dorsal fins of three sharks. "It's okay," Joe said. "I came face-to-face with a shark when I was diving earlier. He didn't bother me at all. Apparently they're mostly dangerous to humans if the humans are near the shore or if the humans are—"

"What is it?" Frank asked, now seeing a stunned look on Joe's face.

"One of us is bleeding," Joe said seriously.

Frank glimpsed a trail of crimson blood in the clear water. "Oh, no," he said. "It must be the cut I got on my ankle from the anchor line. The water probably pulled off my bandage and opened the wound."

Frank knew what Joe had been about to say before he saw the blood. Sharks were only dangerous to humans if the humans were near the shore or *if they were bleeding!* Sharks could smell blood from great distances and would usually go after a bleeding creature.

"Look," Joe said, seeing at least a dozen dorsal fins in the water. They were about a football field away and swimming for the Hardys at a good clip.

"What a day!" Frank cried in frustration.

"This is not good at all," Joe said, trying against all odds to stay cool. "In fact, this is—"

"Shhh," Frank said. "I hear something."

"What is it?" Joe asked, turning.

He saw something silver glinting over a cloud. The silver was a small airplane, and it soon began angling down, heading straight for the Hardys.

"He sees us!" Frank cried out happily. "He's coming down for us!"

"He'd better hurry," Joe said, noticing that the sharks were only about seventy yards away.

The plane was nearing the Hardys, flying close to the water. A side door flew open, the most welcome sight Joe had ever seen. When somebody leaned out of the plane, he was amazed to see it was Jamal.

"Okay, Hardys," Jamal called over the plane's noise. "I'll ask questions later! Here's a rope!" Jamal threw a rope from the plane. The end of it landed nearby and trailed in the water.

"You first," Joe yelled to Frank, seeing the sharks were only fifty yards away.

As the rope approached, swaying back and forth, Frank reached out for it but missed. Then he watched the plane carry the rope farther away, knowing planes, unlike helicopters, couldn't stop their forward motion and hover. Frank had no choice but to float in place while Jamal banked the plane sideways in order to circle back.

Joe took a deep breath. The sharks were maybe a minute away from reaching the Hardys. Joe tried not to imagine how fast their sharp triangular teeth could rip him to shreds.

When Jamal returned, he nosed the plane downward to give Frank more time near the rope. Frank reached for the swaying rope but missed again. As the rope swung back toward him, Frank dived for it, this time grabbing it.

The plane began dragging Frank in a circle through the water as Jamal banked the plane again to return for Joe. While Frank was being pulled, he struggled to shimmy up the rope.

Joe glanced from the plane back to the sharks. Through the crystal-clear water he could see their sleek bluish gray bodies approaching—closer, closer. Thirty seconds, he figured.

Joe turned back to the plane, which was flying right toward him. Frank was dangling from the rope, halfway up, his ankle dripping with blood. Without looking back, Joe knew the sharks were no more than a few yards out.

The rope was swinging wildly from Frank's weight, but Joe knew he had only one shot at it. He knew Jamal would bring the rope as close as possible, and Joe began focusing every inch of his mental power on catching it.

Forget the sharks, Joe thought. Catch the rope. Just catch the rope. Just catch the rope.

The rope swung by—and Joe grabbed it with one hand, then the other.

"Up!" Frank shouted over the plane's buzz. The plane nosed upward, lifting Joe clear out of the water. Gripping the rough fibers of the rope, Joe looked down to see the numerous dorsal fins swimming in circles. He figured the sharks were probably wondering who had stolen their lunch.

As the plane flew slowly forward, Frank and Joe climbed their way up the rope, then Jamal helped pull them into the plane. Jamal was alone in the cramped four-seat cabin, and Frank saw that the end of the rope had been tied around one of the metal seats.

"I saw the flares and went straight for them," Jamal said, returning to the wheel.

"Glad you did," Joe said.

"And I've got a funny feeling something happened to my uncle's boat," Jamal said with a sideways look.

"You know, that old skiff was way past its prime," Frank said, sitting down beside Jamal. "What do you say we buy your uncle a shiny new one?"

"I'd say he'd like that." As Jamal flew the plane back to St. Lucia, the Hardys informed him of everything that had happened. When Jamal flew by the towering Pitons, he acrobatically signed a cursive *J* in the air, his flying signature.

"It always makes me sick to my stomach when you do that," Joe said from the backseat.

"Consider it revenge for the boat," Jamal said with a grin.

Around six the boys returned to the bungalow. Frank and Jamal sat on a worn-out couch drinking coconut soda while Joe made some telephone calls in the kitchen. The soda came in the same brown bottles as Rob and Davy's homemade bombs. Frank decided to put the thought out of his mind.

"Mom and Dad say hi," Joe said, back in the living room. "I told Dad a little about the case but played things down so he wouldn't worry too much."

"If anybody's parents should be used to worrying," Jamal said after a sip of soda, "it's Mr. and Mrs. Fenton Hardy of Bayport."

"Speaking of parents," Frank said, "did you reach Chrissy's folks in Virginia?"

"I sure did," Joe said. "I called the next-of-kin number on that sheet you gave me and got Mrs. Peters, Chrissy's mother. I pretended I was a friend looking for Chrissy. Mrs. Peters said she hasn't spoken to Chrissy in about a month. I poked around some, trying to see if there was any hint of danger or trouble in Chrissy's life, but I didn't find out anything."

"Not that her mother would be the first to know," Frank said, leaning back on the sofa.

"Her mother sounded real friendly," Joe said. "It makes me sick to think any day now she may get a call telling her Chrissy is . . ."

"She won't get that call," Frank said firmly. "We're going to solve this thing, and Chrissy is going to be all right."

"We should probably make some attempt to locate Chrissy," Jamal suggested. "Maybe I'll do that tomorrow while you guys find some other ridiculous situation to—"

The sound of shattering glass cut Jamal off and made everyone jump. A bottle came flying through the living room window. It was another brown coconut soda bottle.

As Joe and Jamal raced outside, Frank picked up the bottle. Instead of soda or gunpowder, the bottle contained a folded piece of paper. Using a pocketknife, Frank pulled the paper out and unfolded it. There was nothing on the paper except a solid black circle, drawn with ink.

"We didn't see anyone," Joe said as he and Jamal breathlessly returned to the room. "The person must have run away real fast or hidden somewhere."

"This was in the bottle," Frank said, showing the paper to Joe and Jamal.

"What does this mean?" Joe asked, puzzled.

"I think I know," Jamal said. "It's a reference to the book *Treasure Island.* When the pirates are planning to kill someone in the book, they first send the victim a 'black spot.' It looks just like this."

"The black spot . . ." Joe said, fishing through his grade-school memories. "I remember that now."

Frank stared at the solid black circle. Someone had marked him and Joe, and possibly Jamal, for death.

9 Green Gold and Real Gold

"Who is planning to kill us?" Joe said, plopping onto the sofa, "or at least threatening to? And why?"

"I don't know who is after us, but I can guess why. Someone knows we're investigating the attempted murder of Chrissy Peters," Frank said, running a hand through his brown hair. "And that someone is telling us to back off."

"Because the person who sent us the black spot," Jamal said, picking up the brown bottle, "is probably the same person who tried to kill Chrissy Peters."

"Right," Frank said.

"How about we get something to eat?" Joe said,

bouncing up from the sofa. "I always get hungry when someone threatens my life."

After the boys showered and changed into long pants and fresh T-shirts, Jamal took the Hardys to the Parrot's Paradise, a small restaurant in Soufrière. Colorful murals were painted on the walls, and fishing nets hung from the ceiling. The place was crowded and loud with chatter.

"Let's review everything we've got so far," Frank said, examining his bowl of Creole goat stew. "Then we'll figure out what the next step should be."

"Our two leading suspects," Joe said, glancing warily at Frank's bowl, "are Pierre Montclare and Peg Riley. We don't have a motive on Montclare, but he was supposedly the last person to see Chrissy before she disappeared. On top of that, he didn't seem to want us on the boat today, and he might have even injured Frank to make his point."

"And don't forget," Frank said after tasting the stew, "he was the one who didn't want to look for Chrissy this morning. He said he didn't want to waste valuable time, but that could have been a lie. This goat stew is delicious, by the way."

"Here's a possible motive," Jamal said, spreading coconut sauce over his grilled fish. "Chrissy was helping Montclare with his books last night. Maybe she found something questionable in his financial records, and Montclare needed to stop her from telling anybody."

"It's not impossible," Joe said, slicing into his jerk chicken, a Caribbean favorite.

"Next suspect," Frank said, "is Peg Riley. She seems nice enough, but we definitely have a motive for her. She's stealing relics from the *Laughing Moon*. Also, Chrissy is Peg's roommate and could easily have found out about this. How's the chicken, Joe?"

"Spicy!" Joe gasped, fanning his mouth.

"Would that alone prompt Peg to kill Chrissy?" Jamal asked.

"It might," Frank answered. "Not only could Peg go to jail, but those items she's stealing are valuable. She could be hoarding thousands of dollars' worth of stuff. People have killed for much less."

"What about Rob and Davy?" Jamal said. "Do they go on the suspect list?"

"They sure do," Frank said. "They asked Flask if they could join the crew if something happened to any of the crew members. Maybe they figured the *Laughing Moon* site was too well guarded for them to get a chance at raiding it. Maybe they saw joining the crew as the only way to get close enough to steal some pirate treasure."

"And they probably came after Frank and me," Joe said, reaching for a plate of fried bananas, "because they thought we were part of the crew."

"So what are you saying?" Jamal asked. "That they tried to kill Chrissy to create an opening on the salvage team? That sounds a bit extreme."

"You should see these guys, Jamal," Joe said with his mouth full. "They're complete lunatics."

"Anyone else?" Frank asked.

"Here's something I just remembered," Joe said. "Ted noticed the oxygen level was low on the *Destiny*'s refill tank today. He wondered if Isaac and Ishmael might be doing some night diving even though they're not supposed to. Maybe they're also stealing stuff from the *Laughing Moon* site, and Chrissy found out about it."

"It's a possibility," Frank said. "I'm getting the impression a lot of secrets are lurking out on Skeleton Reef."

Dusk was deepening into night an hour later as Frank drove the Jeep up a steep hill on the southeastern part of the island. Thunder rumbled above. Over dinner it had been decided that Frank would pay an unexpected visit to Pierre Montclare's house while Joe and Jamal walked to the bungalow where Peg Riley lived. The boys had gotten both addresses off the list Frank had stolen from the *Destiny*.

Rain began to pour on the canvas top of the Jeep. As he turned on the windshield wipers, Frank wondered if the storm was similar to the one that had driven the *Laughing Moon* onto Skeleton Reef so many years ago. It was completely dark when he spotted a lonely house atop a hill. It had to be Montclare's place.

Frank parked in front of the house, a large and elegant structure, then darted through the rain for the front door. He knocked loudly and waited, but there was no answer. Remembering people in the Caribbean did not always lock up, Frank turned the knob and found the door was open. He entered.

The floors of the spacious living room were polished wood, and most of the furniture was wicker. Two fancy floor lamps were casting a halogen glow, suggesting someone was home. "Hello," Frank called out. There was no answer.

Across the room was a door to a veranda, and Frank saw Montclare standing on the veranda, gazing at the torrential rain. Absorbed in thought, Montclare had not heard Frank enter the house. "Excuse me, sir," Frank said, approaching the veranda.

Montclare turned quickly. "What are you doing here?" the dark-haired man asked. Right away, Frank thought there was something troubled or haunted about Montclare's expression.

"I'm real sorry to barge in like this," Frank said, "but, well, it so happens I'm very interested in journalism, and I got to thinking that this whole treasure hunt would make a fabulous story for my high school newspaper. So I, uh, wonder if you could answer a few questions for me."

"I do not like questions," Montclare said with a sigh. "However, I feel bad that I caused you to be injured today, so I will give you a few minutes."

The rain was pounding so loudly on the roof above the veranda that it was difficult to hear.

Frank could see the veranda faced an expanse of large-leafed trees that resembled palms.

"How did you get into the treasure-hunt business?" Frank asked, pulling out a notebook and pen.

"I own a banana plantation," Montclare said, gesturing at the trees. "See, acres and acres of thriving bananas. For a time the plantation was bringing me great profits. In fact, here in the Caribbean, bananas are often referred to as 'green gold.'"

"I didn't know that," Frank said, pretending to drink in every detail.

"Anyway," Montclare continued, "a little over two years ago, Sandy Flask came to St. Lucia. He went around to local businessmen, asking them to invest in his expedition. Everyone refused but me. I had some money to spare, and it sounded like fun, so I agreed to single-handedly finance the treasure hunt. It was agreed that if he found the treasure, which was by no means certain, I would receive fifty percent of the profits. You might say I was financing my search for real gold with green gold."

"It looks as though your gamble is about to pay off," Frank said. "Big time."

"It may," Montclare said with a nod. "But it will be several years before I receive any of the profits. And now that has become a problem for me."

"Why?" Frank asked after a burst of thunder.

"Just recently," Montclare said, "the U.S. and

European markets began purchasing all of their bananas from Central America, and therefore my plantation is now losing money. Also, over the past two years, I have been pouring more and more money into the *Laughing Moon* expedition. I assure you, finding pirate treasure is not a cheap enterprise. So you see, now I am in very bad financial shape."

"I'm sorry to hear that," Frank said.

"Yes," Montclare sad wearily. "Very bad financial shape. I have had to cut back on my staff. Indeed, that is why I hired Chrissy Peters to help me with my books. Because I could no longer afford a full-time accountant. *C'est la vie.*"

"I see," Frank said.

"I'm afraid this financial situation has put me in a very bad temper lately," Montclare said. "That is why I was acting so moody today. Come, let's go inside. I am getting wet."

Frank followed Montclare into the living room, where they both sat in large wicker chairs. Without a word Montclare dropped his head into his hands and began massaging his temples. Frank studied the Frenchman for a few moments. He does seem moody, Frank thought. Am I looking at a man just worried about financial matters, Frank wondered, or am I looking at a man worried about something even more serious—like believing he murdered someone last night?

"Are you all right, sir?" Frank asked.

"No," Montclare muttered, mostly to himself. "I am feeling guilty about something. Mentioning Chrissy just now brought it back to me."

Frank knew a little about psychology. He knew that sometimes people with troubled consciences wanted someone to whom they could confess their crimes. If that's what he wants, Frank thought, I'll give it to him.

"Guilty about what?" Frank asked.

"Something I did last night," Montclare said almost in a whisper.

"What was it?" Frank asked softly.

Montclare lifted his head and stared toward the veranda, watching the rain slash at the banana plantation below. "Last night," Montclare said, slowly forming his words, "Chrissy found some wrongdoing in my records. You see, I was so worried about money, I . . . juggled some things about so I could pay a little less in taxes. Chrissy . . . she . . . she noticed this, and she began teasing me about it."

"So you feel guilty about cheating on your taxes," Frank said, a little disappointed.

"No, not that," Montclare said, turning to face Frank. "I was so uptight about my money problems that I yelled at Chrissy for teasing me. I'm afraid I was quite cross with her. She began crying, and then . . . then she ran out of here."

"You only yelled at her?" Frank asked.

"That is all," Montclare said, looking away. "I

84

fear that is why she did not show up for work this morning. I imagine she wanted to steer clear of me for a few days. Or perhaps she wanted to teach me a lesson by slowing down the expedition. All in all, it is not that momentous a thing, but, still, I feel guilty for hurting her feelings. She is a lovely young woman. Probably the nicest person on the crew."

Frank took all this in, wondering if it was the complete truth. The money part could have been a lie designed to cover Montclare's guilty behavior, and the Chrissy part could have been a lie designed to explain Chrissy's mysterious absence.

"If all that was hurt were her feelings," Frank said, "I'm sure she can forgive you when she returns. That is, if she ever does return."

"I hope so," Montclare said quietly. "Yes, I hope so. Now, please, perhaps you can leave me alone. I . . . I have a little work to do."

"Thank you very much for your time," Frank said. He noticed the rain had stopped as he got up to leave.

Joe and Jamal had ducked into a village pool hall to escape the downpour. Once it had let up, they began walking along a dirt road toward Peg Riley's bungalow. "I think that's it," Jamal said, pointing to a small house peeking through some leaves. The boys walked across the drenched earth to the bungalow, which was surrounded by trees and shrubbery. The paint on the bungalow was peeling badly, and the roof was merely a sheet of corrugated metal, but the address checked out.

No interior lights were on, and no one answered Jamal's knocks at the door. Jamal tried the door, but it was locked. Joe pulled a long piece of metal from the pocket of his khaki pants and slipped it into the front door cylinder. With a few deft turns, he managed to unlock the door.

Joe and Jamal stepped into the darkened bungalow and carefully wiped their feet on a mat. Joe made sure the door was relocked. Then Joe and Jamal flipped on flashlights they had brought from the bungalow. They began to look around, Joe in the living room, Jamal in the bedroom and bathroom.

It seemed the living room was furnished mostly with lawn chairs and milk crates. Joe didn't find any treasure lying around, but then he hadn't expected it to be out in the open. Noticing a book on the floor, he pointed the flashlight on it. His heartbeat sped up when he saw the book was *Treasure Island.*

Then Joe's heart skipped a beat. Someone was unlocking the front door.

10 X Marks the Spot

Joe froze in the dark, trying to figure out what to do, where to hide. He heard the key turning just as Jamal creeped back into the room.

"There's a closet right here," Jamal whispered.

Joe moved toward Jamal's voice, being careful not to bump into anything. Jamal quietly opened the closet door. As the front door swung open, Joe and Jamal stepped into the closet and pulled the door shut. Nice timing, Joe thought.

Joe heard footsteps on the wooden floor. Then he saw a puddle of light spill under the closet door. When he heard the footsteps move farther away, he eased the closet door open a few inches.

Across the room Joe saw Peg Riley. She was standing inside the kitchen, a small area adjoining the living room. Peg was putting on a pair of rubber gloves, the type used for washing dishes. Then Joe noticed a plastic bottle sitting on the kitchen counter. Squinting, he was able to make out the words Muriatic Acid on the bottle.

Peg knelt down and opened the metal cabinet beneath the sink. She pulled two rubber buckets from the cabinet and lifted them to the counter. Then Peg began pulling objects from the buckets.

Joe saw shiny silver coins, half a pewter plate, a tin fork and spoon, fragments of a ceramic teapot, an antiquated pistol, and balls of lead that he assumed were ammunition. Then Peg brought out a necklace composed of gold links. Dangling from it was a medallion shaped like a dragon. The dragon's eyes were two sparkling emeralds, and the dragon was spitting fire simulated by three brilliant rubies.

Joe realized these were relics from the *Laughing Moon,* their encrustation cleaned off from soaking in the acid. He watched Peg fill several clear plastic bags with tap water and pour some salt into each bag. Finally she placed the relics inside the bags and sealed the bags with knots.

Peg picked up the plastic bags, then switched off the kitchen light and carried the bags out the front door. Joe and Jamal waited a moment before stepping out of the closet into the darkened room.

"I think we can sneak out through the bathroom window," Jamal whispered.

88

"Hang on a sec," Joe whispered as he moved to a window in the living room. He wanted to know where Peg was going with the stolen relics. Peeling back a sheet being used as a curtain, Joe peered outside.

Peg was standing by the side of the bungalow, directly in Joe's view. Because the living room was dark, Joe knew it would be difficult for Peg to catch sight of him. The redheaded woman picked up a shovel and began digging.

"What is she doing?" Jamal whispered.

"Believe it or not," Joe whispered back, "I think she's burying the pirate treasure."

Peg dug a small hole in the ground, and Joe could see there were other plastic bags already lying in the moist earth. Peg placed the new plastic bags in the opening, then began shoveling dirt over the hole, her green eyes gleaming with determination.

"X marks the spot," Joe whispered.

"She's probably coming back," Jamal whispered. "Come on, let's hit that bathroom window."

Joe and Jamal carefully made their way across the dark room and entered the bathroom. Joe pulled the door partly shut. The bathroom window seemed large enough for the boys to fit through, and Jamal started to open it. But the window was stuck. Joe helped, but together the boys still could not budge it.

"It's not locked," Jamal whispered, "it's just jammed."

Then Joe heard Peg come into the bungalow.

With a forceful heave, Jamal and Joe pushed up on the window. The window seemed to give just a bit, although it still was not opening. Jamal let out a grunt as he pushed harder. Then he closed his eyes, angry at himself.

Joe and Jamal froze a moment to see if Peg had heard the sound.

"Hello!" Peg yelled from the living room. "Hello! Is anybody there?"

Joe and Jamal looked at each other in tense silence.

"If someone is in this place," Peg called out, "you'd better fess up right now. I've got a bottle of acid in my hand."

Jamal held up his hands to Joe, wondering if they should declare themselves. Joe shook his head. He was thinking. It was a tight spot to be sure, but he had squirmed out of tighter before.

"I'm warning you," Peg called as she drew nearer to the bathroom, "this stuff will burn your face something terrible!"

Jamal looked desperately at Joe.

"Hello!" Peg called, slowly drawing closer. "If someone is there, you'd better tell me right now. I don't like folks barging into my house, and I won't hesitate to throw this acid at you."

As Peg spoke the last few words, Joe gave the window a powerful upward shove. This time the window slid open, the shove timed perfectly so as to be covered by the sound of Peg's voice.

"Hello!" Peg shouted. "Are you in the bathroom? Is that where you are?"

First Jamal, then Joe squeezed out the window. As Peg kept calling, the boys raced across the dampened ground, putting as much distance as they could between themselves and the bottle of acid. When the dense trees finally gave way to the white sand of the beach, Joe and Jamal fell on the ground, panting.

"Hardy," Jamal gasped, "you had me going there for a second."

"Stick with me, Hawkins," Joe replied. "I'll show you every trick in the book."

Joe and Jamal met Frank at ten-thirty in front of the Parrot's Paradise restaurant. The streets were still wet, but the rain looked as if it was gone for the night. A few people were out but not many. As the boys strolled through the village, they brought each other up to date on their recent findings.

"So we know Pierre Montclare feels guilty about something," Joe said. "Maybe it's about yelling at Chrissy and maybe it's about something else."

"Like trying to kill her," Jamal said.

"And we know Peg Riley has stolen pirate loot," Frank said. "And we also know she keeps it at the bungalow where Chrissy was staying."

"In other words," Jamal said, "based on the two encounters we just had, both Montclare and Riley seem even guiltier than before."

"Correct," Frank said. "But we don't have anything conclusive on either one of them. We're still in the realm of guesswork. Which means we need to keep the suspect list open."

Across the street the boys saw a young islander man entertaining a group of tourists. His hair was in dreadlocks, and he was playing a steel drum. Though the drum was fashioned from a beat-up oil barrel, the man made the instrument sing with a sweetly musical sound.

"Let's look at this crime from another angle," Frank said. "Let's go back to the night of the attempted murder. We found Chrissy right by the water, and she later said she had swum a long way. That means she was probably thrown off a boat. Right?"

"Right," Jamal said, tapping his foot to the rhythm of the steel drum. "But anybody can get hold of a boat around here—Montclare, Peg, anybody."

"And let's not forget our theory about Isaac and Ishmael stealing treasure at night," Joe said. "Maybe Chrissy went by the *Destiny* last night for some reason and caught them in the act. Isaac and Ishmael could have thrown her off the *Destiny*."

The boys fell silent a moment, each considering this last option. Joe watched the islander, who was now singing along with his drumming. Joe found the lyrics of the song strangely appropriate.

> "I knew this girl a little while,
> But then she had to go.
> East or west, I can't say which,
> But, oh, I liked her so."

Joe pictured Chrissy in his mind. He saw her lying in the hospital bed with her long chestnut hair draped over the pillow. Then he found himself wondering where she was at the moment. Was she on the island? Was she far away? Was she still alive?

Frank was having similar thoughts about Chrissy and feeling bad that he and Joe had not been able to crack the case yet. Who was after her? And why? And what happened to her the other night? Then he realized something.

"You know," Frank said. "Chrissy couldn't have been thrown off the *Destiny.* The boat is anchored south of where we found her, and the current in the water runs southward. That means it would be impossible for Chrissy to have ended up where we found her. If she was thrown off a boat, and she probably was, it must have been another boat."

"Good point," Joe said. "All the same, I'd like to know if Isaac and Ishmael are stealing treasure. If they are, we should definitely find a way to investigate them further. Maybe they've even got a racket going with Peg."

"Here's an idea," Jamal said. "The weather seems to have cleared up. Why don't I pick up my uncle's plane and we can fly over the *Destiny* tonight? If Isaac and Ishmael are diving for treasure at night, they'll need to have lights in the water. We should be able to spot the lights from the air. What do you say?"

"I say you're an awfully handy fellow to have around, Jamal," Frank said. "Let's do it."

The boys drove to the southern tip of the island, where the airport was located. Jamal filed a flight plan and carefully checked the Cessna-172 plane that belonged to his uncle. Moments later he expertly guided the plane into the sky. The boys wore headsets with microphones so they could communicate over the engine noise. Lights twinkled around the perimeter of the island, most of the hotels and larger villages being near the shore.

Soon the plane was droning over the dark and peaceful Caribbean Sea. Seated next to Jamal, Frank was drawing lines on the map as he continually checked the plane's compass. Through a cloud, Joe glimpsed the ghostlike outline of a crescent moon. "Are we close to the ship?" Joe asked from the backseat.

"In less than a minute," Frank spoke into his mike, "we should be right over the *Destiny*."

A minute passed, but the boys saw no sign of the *Destiny* at the dive site. There was nothing beneath the plane's wings but the dark expanse of sea. Jamal flew the Cessna up and down the general area in case Frank's calculations had been slightly off.

"There's nothing down there but water and more water," Jamal told Frank after several minutes of reconnaissance. "Your navigation may have been a little faulty, but we've combed the entire southern section of the reef."

"This is very puzzling," Frank said, rubbing his forehead. "Let's go back to my first guess."

Jamal banked the plane and circled back to the site where Frank originally thought the *Destiny* should have been located. This time Jamal flew the plane lower and switched on the landing lights. The boys carefully watched the water, which was now illuminated by a strong beam of light coming from the Cessna.

"Look to the right!" Joe called, peering out his window.

Frank looked down and spotted a bright orange plastic buoy floating in the water, and he noticed there was a black skull and crossbones painted on it. "That should be the right spot," Frank said, glancing at his map. "Maybe Flask moved the boat and left the buoy as a marker."

"I seriously doubt it," Joe said. "Flask told us the *Destiny* always stays on the treasure site. He knows if he moves the boat, there's a chance someone will come in at night and raid the place."

"Then what could have happened to the boat?" Jamal asked, banking the plane to circle back.

"Maybe the ghost of Rebecca took it," Joe joked, tilting sideways with the banking plane.

"I might agree with you," Jamal said as he leveled the plane, "except she wouldn't have left a buoy to mark the spot, would she?"

"I'm afraid we're faced with only one conclusion," Frank said thoughtfully. "Someone has stolen, or at least borrowed, the *Destiny*."

"Who would do that?" Joe asked.

"I don't know," Frank said, looking at the black skull and crossbones on the buoy. "But I've got a feeling these waters hold a lot of secrets."

11 Something Fishy

"Why don't I fly around, and maybe we'll spot the *Destiny* somewhere else," Jamal said.

"Just don't try any more of those fancy acrobatics," Joe said. "My stomach is still pretty full from dinner."

"I won't, Ace," Jamal promised.

As Jamal flew the plane north, Joe spotted a luxury yacht on the water. "Sometimes I think it would be nice to be rich," he said, watching a group of people partying on the deck.

"Rich people have problems, too," Frank said, studying his map. "Look at Pierre Montclare."

"You mean the banana man?" Jamal said humorously.

After seeing the yacht the boys saw no other

vessels on the water for a while. On the map Frank saw the southern section of Skeleton Reef, where the *Destiny* was supposed to be anchored. There was a gap between the southern and northern sections of the reef.

"Take a look at two o'clock," Joe said as the plane flew above the northern section.

Up ahead, slightly to the right, Frank spotted a vessel that resembled the *Destiny*. As the plane flew closer, he glimpsed a Jolly Roger flag on the masthead. "Bingo," Frank said. "That's her."

Near the port side of the boat, Joe saw a dim glow of light in the darkened sea. "I think that's a diving light in the water," he said as the Cessna passed over the top of the *Destiny*. "Do you see anyone on deck?"

"Not yet," Frank answered.

"I'll take us back around," Jamal said. "Look hard, though, because I don't want to turn the landing lights on. No point in giving ourselves away."

Jamal flew the Cessna in a wide, easy circle over the *Destiny*. Watching closely through the window, Frank saw two muscular men sitting on the *Destiny*'s top deck. "Yup, that's definitely Isaac and Ishmael down there," Frank said.

"Do you think they're the ones doing the diving?" Jamal asked.

"I doubt it," Frank said, his head pressed against

his window. "The lights are still in the water, but Isaac and Ishmael aren't wearing any scuba gear. They seem to be just hanging out. I would guess there are one or more other people in the water right now."

"I wonder who," Joe said.

"That's just one more underwater secret," Frank said. "Jamal, make another circle. I want to see if anyone else is anywhere on deck."

"I'll fly a bit lower," Jamal said. "Maybe they'll think we're just interested in getting a look at the boat with the nifty pirate flag."

As Jamal continued banking the plane in a wide circle, he angled down to a slightly lower altitude. Frank scanned the entire *Destiny* in search of somebody new but saw no other people above decks. Then, as Frank's eyes roamed back over the top deck, he saw that Isaac and Ishmael were aiming rifles at the Cessna.

"Jamal, watch it!" Frank exclaimed. "They're pointing rifles at us!"

Two gunshots pierced the peaceful night.

Jamal spun the wheel, banking the plane until it was almost flying on its side.

"What are you doing?" Joe shouted, slamming against the side of the cabin.

"He's narrowing their target," Frank said. "If a bullet hits us in the wrong place, we could be in big trouble."

Two more shots exploded. Joe winced when he heard a bullet *ching* against the wing beneath him. "I think one hit the port wing!" he shouted.

"That should be okay," Jamal said. "Hang on!" He quickly leveled out the plane, but just as Frank and Joe returned to normal positions, Jamal pulled back on the wheel and sent the plane angling steeply upward. Joe felt his stomach doing a backflip as the plane swiftly ascended.

"You can relax now," Jamal said as he leveled the plane again. "We're out of gunshot range."

"Well, we got some acrobatics after all," Joe said as his stomach slowly settled.

"They must have suspected we were snooping on them," Jamal said, flying the plane away from the *Destiny.* "Fortunately they have no way of knowing who was in the plane."

"Don't be so sure," Frank told the others. "One of the people on or under the *Destiny* might be the person who sent us the black spot a few hours ago. He might be keeping track of our every move."

"There's something fishy going on down there," Joe said, looking back at the distant spot where the water faintly glowed.

"Fishy is right," Frank said. "But what is it?"

"For some reason," Jamal said as he veered the plane eastward, "some people are moving the *Destiny* to the northern section of Skeleton Reef. And they're diving there. Why? For recreation? Doubtful. They're probably looking for something on that part of the reef."

"Remember when we met Ted last night?" Joe said. "He mentioned there were plenty of wrecks out here. Maybe there's another pirate ship down below. Or maybe another kind of boat sank with valuable cargo. And from what I understand, you need government permission to go digging in the reef. So whoever is diving off the *Destiny* right now may actually be committing a crime."

"If something illegal is going on down there, and Chrissy found out about it . . ." Frank paused, then said excitedly, "Wait. If last night the *Destiny* was where we just saw it, Chrissy could have been thrown off the ship and ended up where we found her. The *Destiny* is now north of where Chrissy washed up, and, as I said earlier, the current runs southward. This is all hypothetical, of course, but it's food for thought."

"Yes, it is," Joe remarked. "Real fishy food."

Minutes later Jamal glided in for a landing at the airport. After touching down, he taxied the Cessna from the runway to a concrete strip where most of the lightplanes were parked. Several metal airplane hangars stood on one side of the strip, and a forest of green vegetation loomed on the other side.

The boys climbed from the Cessna, and Joe noticed the only people in the area were two men standing by a deluxe lightplane parked at the opposite end of the strip. Something about one of the men caught Joe's eye. "Hey," he told Frank, "isn't that Sandy Flask over there?"

"It sure is," Frank said.

Frank, Joe, and Jamal watched the two men a few moments. Flask was talking with a silver-haired man in a navy blazer and white pants. The captain opened a battered suitcase and pulled out several clear plastic bags. Flask opened one of the bags and lifted a small object out of it. The object glittered in a spill of light cast by an overhead lamppost.

"That's gold!" Jamal exclaimed. "Nothing else catches the light that way. Could that be something from the *Laughing Moon* site?"

"It shouldn't be," Frank said. "Flask isn't allowed to take anything found on the site. The archaeologist is supposed to be in charge of everything."

"That didn't stop Peg Riley," Joe said. "Come on. I want a closer look."

Joe led Frank and Jamal into the dense region of trees and shrubbery just beyond the concrete. Camouflaged by the greenery, the boys walked a short distance, then hid in the trees not far from where Flask and the man were standing.

Flask was pulling objects from the bags and laying them on the airplane wing. Joe saw gold and silver coins, gold ingots, fragments of a teapot, an antiquated pistol, balls of lead, a gold chain with a dragon medallion. "Whoa," Joe whispered. "Some of that stuff is what I saw Peg Riley burying tonight."

"Why would Flask have it?" Frank asked.

"Maybe Peg was stealing the booty for him," Joe said. "Maybe Flask doesn't want to play by the government's rules and wait several years before any of the relics can be sold. After all, he's already poured four years of his life into finding the *Laughing Moon* site. And maybe he's not too thrilled about getting only twenty percent of the profits."

"Do you really think he would steal from his own expedition?" Frank asked, keeping his eyes on the pirate treasures. The man with silver hair was examining them, obviously impressed.

"Just because he's a captain doesn't mean he can't be greedy," Joe said. "In fact, he probably feels he has more right to those relics than anybody."

"And you said the guy is obsessed with pirates," Jamal said. "Maybe the old geezer is something of a pirate himself. You know, he kind of looks like one."

"Or maybe we're jumping to some big conclusions here," Frank said.

Flask turned suddenly and looked right in the direction where Jamal and the Hardys were hiding.

"Shhh," Jamal said. "Nobody move."

"We're not," Frank whispered back.

Flask was scanning the greenery as if searching for an enemy ship on the horizon, and Frank had a

103

feeling that Flask's experienced eyes never missed a trick. "Peekaboo, I see you," Flask called after a few moments. "Now, why don't you fellows come out of there? Whoever you are."

"Stay," Joe whispered to his companions. "If he wants to come for us, let him. We've got him outnumbered."

"Maybe you didn't hear me," Flask called again. "Maybe I need to speak a little louder." Flask reached around to the back of his pants and pulled out a small automatic pistol. "Now step on out of there, you rascals," Flask ordered. "Immediately!"

He released the safety catch on the pistol and aimed the weapon at Joe.

12 Why Pirates Were Pirates

"Don't shoot!" Joe called. He stepped from behind a tree with his hands in the air.

"Hardy?" Flask said, surprised. "Funny seeing you here. Now tell your friends to step out or else my trigger finger might get a sudden itch."

Frank and Jamal stepped out from their hiding places with their hands in the air. The man with the silver hair was nervously watching the scene.

"Dandy," Flask said, keeping the pistol trained on Joe. "Now how about somebody telling me what's going on?"

"Our friend Jamal here," Frank explained, "has access to a plane and we were out for a night flight."

"Yeah," Flask said, swinging the gun to Frank. "But then why were you dogs spying on me?"

"I was getting to that," Frank said calmly. "You see, after we parked our plane, we saw you showing some things to that man. And, uh, we were curious about what you were showing him."

"Did you see what I was showing?" Flask asked.

"Not really," Frank said.

"Hardy, I don't believe you," Flask said, almost growling. "Try telling me the truth!"

Frank knew Flask was a man who didn't like to be bamboozled, and he decided to play it straight. "You were showing that man relics from the *Laughing Moon*," he said.

"That's better." Flask smiled. "And I bet you boys think I've stolen these relics, don't you?"

"Nobody said that," Joe said.

"Well, I *have* stolen them," Flask said. "And just now I thought you kids were trying to filch them from me. But I see I was mistaken."

"I'm glad you see that," Jamal said.

Flask lowered the pistol, flipped the safety on, and stuffed the gun back into his pants. With relief, the boys lowered their hands. The man with silver hair began mopping his face with a handkerchief.

"Hey, Nelson!" Flask said, turning to the man. "Keep a close eye on that booty. I'll be with you in just a few." Nelson waved his hand, and Flask walked over to the boys.

"Sir," Joe said, "may we ask why you stole those relics?"

"Well"—Flask shoved back a lock of his scraggly hair— "since you boys have found me out, I guess I have to let you in on my little secret."

"Another secret," Jamal muttered.

"Follow me," Flask said.

With the boys behind him, Flask walked through the leafy vegetation until he came to a high ledge overlooking the southern tip of the island.

"As soon as we started pulling those beautiful doodads out of the sand," Flask said, staring out to sea, "I knew it wasn't right to sell them for a profit. I told myself, Sandy, old boy, that stuff belongs in a museum. A place that's a lot of fun to visit but where people can also learn the truth about pirates."

"What *is* the truth about pirates?" Joe asked, eyeing Flask suspiciously. "Besides the fact that they liked to shoot cannons and rob other ships."

"Oh, there's a lot more to it than that," Flask said. "In their own crude way, they were revolutionaries. Back in those days, most folks were terribly poor, and there was no democracy anywhere. What the pirates really wanted was some equality. The pirates didn't start stealing because they were greedy. No, sir. They started stealing because they were starving."

"Is that right?" Joe asked.

"Yup," Flask said. "And those pirate ships were

democratic in most every way. Men of all races were treated alike. The captains were voted in, and if they weren't good leaders, they were voted out. They say Black Dan Cavendish was one of the best. Supposedly the day he became a pirate captain, he climbed the rigging of his ship and proclaimed, 'Brothers, never again will you be captives of the wealthy. From this day forth you are free men!'"

"I never knew any of this," Joe said.

"Me, either," Frank added.

"Well, then, there ought to be a pirate museum," Jamal said. "Personally, I would love to see it."

"The problem is this," Flask said, scratching his chin. "Pierre Montclare owns fifty percent of whatever we find, and he doesn't go for the museum idea. When I asked him about it, he said he needed to sell his share of the relics to help him out of a bad financial situation. A museum could take years to start turning a profit."

"So why don't you get somebody to buy out Montclare's share?" Frank asked. "That way Montclare gets money right now and you get your museum."

"That's exactly what I'm trying to do," Flask replied. "Nelson back there is a wealthy businessman who is considering the possibility of the museum. You see, I needed to have the relics in hand to show to potential investors."

"Why couldn't you just take the potential backers out on the *Destiny*?" Frank asked. "That way they could see the stuff without all this sneaking around."

"Some days we find a lot of incredible things," Flask said, "and some days we hardly find anything. And these business types don't have several days to kill hanging around on a boat."

"Couldn't you just borrow some of the pirate stuff to show the potential backers?" Jamal asked.

"Nope," Flask said, after spitting on the ground. "I asked the government archaeologist about that, but he nixed the idea real fast. Understandably, he's paranoid about those valuable items getting stolen."

"So how did you get all that stuff in the bags?" Joe asked.

"Like I said, I stole them," Flask said with a grin. "Or to be more specific, I had Peg Riley steal them. Every now and then, she smuggles out a few choice items and takes them to her place. Then she cleans off the encrustation and buries everything in a secret spot. When I need the stuff, I come by and pick it up. I know it's all a bit pirate-like, but then maybe that's why I like it."

"What will you do with the stolen items once you find an investor?" Joe asked.

"I'll return every bit of it to the common pot," Flask said emphatically. "Much as I like pirates, I'm not a thief myself."

"One more question," Frank said. "Why the gun?"

"Son," Flask answered, "the stuff I'm carrying tonight is probably worth a hundred thousand dollars. And don't forget, those fools Rob and Davy are lurking around. As a matter of fact, at first I thought you guys were them. You're probably lucky I didn't blow you to smithereens."

"I'm counting my blessings," Jamal said.

"Have you heard anything about Chrissy Peters?" Joe asked.

"Not a peep," Flask said, a serious look in his eyes. "It's the strangest thing, her disappearing like that. She's an awfully sweet kid, and I sure hope she's okay."

"So do we," Frank said, looking out at the dark sea below. "Wherever she is."

"Well, I'd better get back to Nelson," Flask said as he cracked his knuckles. "He seems pretty keen on the museum idea, and I don't want to keep him waiting. Can I rely on you fellows to guard my secret?"

"Yes, sir," Joe said with a salute. "We're good with secrets."

"I'm glad to hear it," Flask said, tipping his cap. "And maybe I'll see you three at my pirate museum one day. Okay, mates, yo ho ho and a bottle of coconut soda!" Then, with a gruff chuckle, Flask began tramping back toward the airport.

"Was he telling the truth?" Jamal asked.

"My gut instinct says yes," Frank said.

"Well, if he was telling the truth," Joe said, "that

means Peg probably wasn't the one who tried to kill Chrissy Peters. If Chrissy had caught Peg stealing, Peg would just have explained the situation to Chrissy. And I imagine Chrissy would have understood."

"I think," Jamal said, "we should focus our attention on finding out what those guys on the *Destiny* might be looking for on the northern part of the reef. If it turns out to be something really important, I would move them, whoever they are, into the position of chief suspects."

"I agree." Frank checked his watch. "It's already well past midnight. Maybe we should turn in and get a fresh start tomorrow."

"I'm for that," Joe said, covering a yawn. "I've never had such an exhausting vacation!"

The sun blazed brightly the following morning as Joe drove the Jeep down one of the island's many green slopes. Jamal's mission for the day was to rent a car and comb the island for a sign of Chrissy. Frank and Joe were headed for a library in Castries, a village on the northeastern part of the island, where they hoped to find a clue to what somebody might be looking for on the northern end of Skeleton Reef.

At the library the Hardys spent three hours leafing through newspapers, recent books, and old leather-bound volumes. Though the brothers found plenty of information on ships that had passed through the area over the years, they failed to find the significant clue they were looking for.

"I don't know if we're going to find anything this way," Joe said, wearily rubbing his eyes. "It took Flask a year of bookwork to get a rough idea of where the *Laughing Moon* might be. I wish somebody could tell us what might be out there on the northern part of the reef."

"Wait," Frank said, slowly closing a book. "Maybe somebody can."

"Like who?" Joe asked.

"Auntie Samantha," Frank said. "Remember, she said she knew everything about this island. And she told us just where to find her."

"Inside the volcano," Joe said, excited. "How could we forget an address like that?"

"Right," Frank said, scooting his chair out. "So let's go find the volcano."

Soon the Hardys were back in the Jeep, driving up and down the green slopes, heading toward the volcano known as La Soufrière. Though Frank was consulting a map, the dirt roads had no signs. Before long the Hardys were hopelessly lost on a desolate part of the island where there was less vegetation and no trace of people. For almost thirty minutes the Hardys looked for someone to give them directions.

Finally Joe pulled the Jeep over and spotted an elderly man climbing a hill. The man was in the company of a mule, and Frank could see a few shacks on the grassy hilltop. Frank and Joe began climbing after the man. The day had turned hot, and soon the brothers were sweating and swatting mosquitoes as they made their way upward.

"Hi, there," Frank called as the Hardys approached the man. "We're looking for La Soufrière, the volcano. Could you tell us how to get there?"

The man stopped, and the mule eyed the Hardys suspiciously. "Sure," the man said, his face shaded by a straw hat. "I write it down for you." Frank handed the man a pen and paper.

"Mind if I pet the mule?" Joe asked.

"Better not," the man said. "Sometimes she like to bite tourists."

"Oh," Joe said, putting his hands in his pockets.

The man handed Frank the sheet of paper. "Thanks," Frank said, noticing the instructions were mostly drawings with pointing arrows.

"No sweat, mon," the man said with a wave. Then he and the mule continued trudging up the hill.

The Hardys quickly descended. At the foot of the hill, they passed three skinny white goats grazing in the grass. "They must belong to the folks who live in the shacks," Frank said as the Hardys continued toward the Jeep. "The goats are probably their source of milk and meat."

"It might be kind of nice living out here," Joe said, wiping sweat from his brow. "You know, a complete escape from the twentieth century."

"First you want to live on a yacht," Frank said, turning to his brother, "and now you want to live with a bunch of goats. Joe, sometimes I wonder—"

Frank stopped, feeling something skim the top of his head. Looking behind him, he saw an object shoot into the bark of a tree. It was a long metal rod with a sharpened tip, the type of spear shot from a speargun.

Frank whipped around and peered at the surrounding trees. He saw no sign of anyone—but someone definitely had him in his sights. Another spear whizzed straight for his face at lightning speed!

13 Inside the Volcano

Frank dropped to the ground. The spear fell several feet behind him.

"What's going on?" Joe asked, squatting beside his brother.

"Someone over by the goats is shooting a spear-gun at us," Frank said urgently. "And careful, the spears are hard to see."

Shielding his eyes from the glare, Joe saw the three goats still grazing by the trees. All he heard was the buzzing of insects.

Then the buzzing was mixed with a whizzing sound, and the next second Joe felt a prick on his forearm. A long metal spear slid onto the grass behind him. He had been grazed by the spear point.

"We're sitting ducks right here!" Frank yelled, getting up from the ground. "Head for the Jeep."

Frank and Joe raced through the grass, soon coming to the dirt road where the Jeep was parked. Both boys jumped into the Jeep. As Joe turned the key in the ignition, Frank heard another spear clang against the Jeep's rear fender. Frank glanced back, but all he saw were trees and grass and goats.

Joe hit the accelerator, and with a jolt the Jeep barreled down the dirt road. "Someone almost turned me into shish kebab!" he exclaimed.

"You're not the only one," Frank said.

"Who do you think it was?" Joe asked.

"Probably the person who sent us the black spot," Frank said, turning to watch the road behind them. "Someone must have been tailing us most of the morning, waiting for a chance to get off a few shots at us. I don't see anyone following us now, though."

"Today is Saturday," Joe said as he guided the Jeep down a steep slope. "That's the *Destiny* crew's day off. So it could easily have been a member of the crew. Also, I remember seeing a few spearguns on the *Destiny.*"

"And I remember Lou Brunelli giving himself a manicure with a spear," Frank said.

A mile later Joe slowed the Jeep down as the dirt road began curving into a serpentine pattern. Then he heard an engine some distance behind.

116

The engine was getting louder a little too fast. Frank saw a brown Jeep swing around a curve and come roaring for the Hardys, stirring up a thick cloud of brown dust. Two men were in the Jeep, but the top was up and Frank couldn't make out the faces.

Though the road was very narrow, the brown Jeep was gunning for the Hardys with no sign of slowing.

"Watch out!" Frank called.

Joe glimpsed the Jeep in his rearview mirror. Then it was careening wildly alongside Joe, the engine thundering in his ear.

Joe swerved to the right to avoid collision as the brown Jeep catapulted ahead.

"Watch it starboard!" Frank cried out. Seeing he was about to fly off the road into a ravine, Joe swerved the Jeep back to the left.

The sound of raucous laghter came pouring from the Jeep. Two heads popped out of the windows for a look back, but Frank didn't need to see the faces. The laughter was enough.

"Guess who?" Frank told Joe.

"Good old Rob and Davy," Joe said with a smirk.

Rob and Davy disappeared around a curve, their insane laughter fading in the distance.

"It seems they like destroying Jeeps as much as destroying boats," Frank said, wiping dust from his eyes.

"Or maybe it's just us they want to destroy," Joe said. "Do you think they were the ones with the speargun?"

"Actually I don't," Frank said. "The person shooting those spears didn't want to be seen. But that's not Rob and Davy's style. If anything, they're rather proud of their wicked ways. I think meeting Rob and Davy today may just have been some bad luck."

"In other words, they would have run this Jeep down no matter who was in it," Joe said.

"As Sandy Flask told us," Frank said, "they're just plain crazy."

"Well, here's the deal," Joe said, easing the Jeep along another curve. "It seems whoever went after Chrissy Peters is starting to come after us—with an intention to kill. We better find out who it is, and soon, or we may never get off this island alive."

As the day eased into late afternoon, the Hardys finally passed a sign that read: La Soufrière, the World's Only Drive-Through Volcano. Joe pulled into a dirt parking lot, where a number of other cars were gathered. A man informed the Hardys they had to hire a guide if they wished to enter the volcano, then pointed to a group of guides standing at the edge of the lot.

"Look, there's Auntie Samantha," Frank said, seeing the elderly lady among the guides.

"Hi," Joe said as the brothers approached Auntie Samantha. "Remember us?"

"Of course I remember you," Auntie Samantha said, adjusting the bandanna on her head. "I told you about Rebecca the other night. Would you like to see the volcano? In addition to being a storyteller, I am also one of the guides."

"Sure," Frank said, reaching in his pocket for money to pay Auntie Samantha's fee.

Auntie Samantha led the boys up a small hill and down the other side. Soon Frank felt as if he had set foot on a distant planet. All around, the landscape was composed of rough grayish black rock that rose and fell with complete irregularity. In various areas, steam was rising from the rocks, and Frank detected the rotten-egg smell of sulphur.

"You are now standing inside the crater of a volcano," Auntie Samantha explained as the Hardys watched in fascination. "No longer does this volcano erupt, but it still simmers and stews. Stay close to me as we walk or you may step in a very hot place."

Frank noticed a few other tourists being led through the crater by guides. Not far away, he saw a car driving slowly along the barren surface.

Auntie Samantha led the Hardys along the rocks a ways, then stopped. Near his feet, Frank saw a pool of black goo, bubbling from the geothermal heat of the earth. "This is pretty cool," he said.

"I wonder if we could install one of these in the backyard," Joe said, watching the black bubbles glurp up and down in the goo.

119

"All right, back to business," Frank said after giving Joe a quizzical look. "Auntie Samantha, we have a question for you. You said you know most everything about this island, and we need to know something about Skeleton Reef."

"Of course," Auntie Samantha replied. "What is it you need to know?"

"We're wondering if there might be a boat or ship that sank on the northern part of the reef. Not just any vessel, though. A vessel that went down with some kind of unusual or valuable cargo."

Auntie Samantha looked at Frank with a somber expression. A long moment passed as he heard only the goo gurgling in the ground and waited for the elderly woman's response.

"Yes," Auntie Samantha said finally. "There is something evil on that part of the reef. Quite evil indeed."

"Like what?" Joe asked.

"I am sorry," Auntie Samantha answered, "but I cannot tell you. It is a secret."

"Auntie Samantha," Frank persisted, "I can't tell you why exactly, but it is very important we know what that evil thing is. A person's life may depend on it. I mean that literally."

Auntie Samantha looked at Frank, then Joe, studying their faces. "All right," she said, "I have decided to trust you. You seem to be honest and good boys."

"That's us," Joe said. "Honest and good."

As Auntie Samantha continued walking along the rocky ground, Frank and Joe followed. "Do you know what plutonium is?" Auntie Samantha asked the boys.

"Sure," Frank said. "It's a radioactive element that's extremely rare. It's noted for being one of the only two substances that can fuel a nuclear bomb."

"That is right," Auntie Samantha said. "Now, in the early 1960s, the Russian government sent some plutonium to Cuba. It was only a small quantity but enough to make two nuclear bombs."

"Did Cuba make the bombs?" Joe asked, passing another pool of the bubbling black goo.

"No," Auntie Samantha said as the rocky path inclined upward. "When the Russian ship bringing the plutonium docked in Cuba, the Russians handed over the box containing the plutonium to the Cuban officials. But someone on that ship had already moved the plutonium into a crate of wheat that was one of many crates also being brought to Cuba. You see, it was all part of a plan to keep Cuba from getting the plutonium."

"What happened to the crate of wheat?" Joe asked, waving some sulphurous vapor away from his face.

"One of the Cubans who was unloading the supply crates," Auntie Samantha continued, "took that crate of wheat with the plutonium and put it in his truck. Then he drove to the other side of the island. There he gave the crate to a fisherman, who put it on a fishing boat called *El Gato*. That is Spanish for 'the cat.'"

"Why were these people stealing the plutonium from Cuba?" Frank asked as a group of tourists walked by with their guide.

"This I am not sure about," Auntie Samantha said. "Some say they were planning to sell it for a lot of money. Others say they were working for the United States CIA, who very much did not want the Cubans to have atomic bombs."

"What happened once the plutonium was on *El Gato*?" Frank asked.

Auntie Samantha paused to rest. The vaporous mist was much thicker now, which made the sulphurous smell all the stronger. Glancing at one of the nearby pools, Frank saw its goo was yellow and bubbled more intensely than the black.

"*El Gato* was on its way to the coast of Brazil," Auntie Samantha explained. "But in the Caribbean Sea, *El Gato* hit a big storm, and like many other boats through the years, it sank on Skeleton Reef. Right on the northern edge. The plutonium and all but one of the men ended up at the bottom of the sea."

"One man survived?" Joe asked.

"Yes," Auntie Samantha said. "He swam to the shore of St. Lucia."

"So that plutonium might still be on the reef?" Frank asked.

"I am fairly sure it is," Auntie Samantha said.

"It sounds like a pretty far-fetched story," Joe said. "Are you sure it's true?"

"What you say, boy?" Auntie Samantha said as if deeply offended. "All my stories are true!"

"I'm sure they are," Frank said with a smile. "But are you sure this one is really, really true?"

"Yes, I am," Auntie Samantha said gravely.

"How do you know?" Frank asked.

"Because," Auntie Samantha said, gesturing with her hands, "the man who swam to the shore became the husband of a woman who was the sister-in-law of a friend of a cousin of my very own mother."

"Oh," Frank replied.

"Can't really argue with that, can we?" Joe concluded.

The Hardys followed as Auntie Samantha resumed climbing upward on the rocks. "I know the story is true," Auntie Samantha said, huffing as she climbed, "but I keep it a deep secret because I don't want anybody looking for that plutonium. It is valuable enough so that others may want it, and it is dangerous enough to cause the deaths of many many people."

"Who else knows about the plutonium?" Joe asked.

"A few islanders know," Auntie Samantha replied, "but they also keep it a secret. And I told one other person about it recently."

"Who?" Joe asked, wiping sweat from his neck.

Auntie Samantha and the Hardys stopped. They were higher up, and Frank could see most of the crater area. With mist rising and swirling from the rocky crags in all directions, the crater looked like the set of a Hollywood horror movie.

"I told that man who is digging up the *Laughing Moon*," Auntie Samantha said. "Sandy Flask."

"Why did you tell Flask?" Frank asked.

"Because I know he is good at finding things in the sea and pulling them out," she explained. "Also he seemed like someone I could trust. I told him about the plutonium because I want him to pull it up and give it to me. Then I'll bury it in a place nobody knows about but Auntie Samantha. When I die, it will be gone forever. All this because that plutonium is evil, evil, evil!"

Suddenly there was an intense hissing sound, and Frank turned to see a geyser of the yellowish goo spraying furiously into the air.

"Stand back," Auntie Samantha said. "That stuff is more than boiling hot!"

"Did Flask agree to find the plutonium?" Joe asked, taking a few steps back.

"He say he was too busy right now!" Auntie Samantha shouted over the hissing. "But he said he would consider it when he had some extra time."

"I see," Frank said, watching the geyser subside as suddenly as it had sprayed. "Well, Auntie Samantha, you've been really helpful to us. We paid you for the tour, but can we pay you a little extra for the story?"

"No, this one is for free," Auntie Samantha said with a friendly wink. "I like you boys."

Soon the Hardys were back in the Jeep, driving toward the bungalow. "Do you think Flask is using the *Destiny* to look for that plutonium at night?" Joe asked as he steered.

"Not Flask," Frank said. "He wasn't on the *Destiny* last night, and, as you said, I don't think he would risk moving the boat. But Flask may have told some of the crew about the plutonium, and some of them might be looking for it without telling him."

"Obviously Isaac and Ishmael are involved," Joe said, shifting gears as he drove up a slope. "And we know they aren't the only ones because someone with them was in the water last night."

"They're probably looking to sell the plutonium, for a lot of money," Frank said. A grapefruit-size quantity of plutonium is enough to power a bomb that can destroy the better part of a city. As Auntie Samantha said, that stuff is evil. Even if the divers find half that amount, they could probably make several million dollars off it."

"Digging on the reef without permission is illegal," Joe said. "And selling plutonium is even more illegal. If Chrissy found out about the scheme— overheard something, saw something—then the guys looking for the plutonium would have a strong motive for getting rid of her."

"Or, then again," Frank said, "maybe Chrissy knows nothing about the plutonium scheme."

Twilight had descended on the island by the time the Hardys pulled up beside the bungalow. Finding the house empty, the brothers walked down to the beach to see if Jamal was there. The sky was veiled with a pastel layer of pink and orange, and the sun was just touching the rim of the sea.

When they reached the sand, the Hardys saw a young woman standing in the shallow part of the water. She wore a loose white caftan that billowed gently in the breeze. She was gazing out at the water with her back to the Hardys. Frank was not the superstitious type, but by the eerie light of dusk the young woman resembled nothing so much as a ghost.

"Who is that?" Frank said quietly.

"It looks like Rebecca," Joe whispered in awe.

14 Return of the Ghost

"Wait," Frank said, squinting to see the young woman better. "That's not Rebecca. It's Chrissy!"

"You're right!" Joe cried with joy. He realized the long chestnut hair was the same he had seen draped over the hospital pillow. Joe had never been so happy to see someone he hardly knew.

"And there's Jamal under that palm tree," Frank said. "He must have found her. Come on."

Frank and Joe hurried over to Jamal, who was sitting on the sand watching Chrissy. "Well, you must have done something right," Joe said.

"Not really," Jamal said, standing up. "I went through several villages asking about Chrissy but didn't find a thing. About a half hour ago, I came here. There I saw her, wading through the water.

I explained how we've been trying to help her out."

"Where has she been?" Frank asked.

"After she escaped from the hospital," Jamal explained, "she hopped a plane to the island of Grenada. She hid out there all say yesterday, then decided to come back here today."

"Did she tell you what happened to her?" Joe asked, stealing a glance at Chrissy. "It's getting more and more important that we find out who tried to murder her. We might be next on the list."

"No," Jamal said, shaking his head. "She doesn't remember. It's as if she's blocked the whole thing out of her mind. That's why she came back to St. Lucia; she thought being here would help release her memory. She's walking the beach right now to try to remember what happened to her Thursday night."

After the Hardys described the day's adventures to Jamal, the boys walked over to Chrissy, stopping where the water met the shore. Chrissy turned to face the Hardys, her long hair blowing in the breeze. "Hello," Frank said. "It's good to see you."

"Same here," Chrissy said a bit shyly. She seemed worried.

"Are you having any luck with your memory?" Joe asked.

"Not really," Chrissy answered with a sigh. "I'm fairly certain somebody tried to kill me Thursday night. But everything else about that night, and even the few days before it, is a complete blank."

"You've probably blocked out everything surrounding that event," Frank said, "because it was so terrifying. People do that sometimes."

"Does being here on the beach help any?" Joe asked, folding his arms on his chest.

"I feel as if it's bringing the memories closer," Chrissy said. "But still not close enough."

"Come here," Frank said, leading Chrissy to a spot on the sand beneath a cluster of palm trees. Joe and Jamal followed, and everyone sat. Joe felt a cool current of air as the palm leaves rustled overhead. Gazing at the sea, he saw the twilight sky was now dramatically streaked with purple and lavender.

"Chrissy," Frank said, his brown eyes focusing on the girl, "I'm going to try to help you remember. Please, just relax. Now, Thursday night you helped Pierre Montclare with his bookkeeping. You were at his plantation house. Do you remember that?"

"No," Chrissy said, looking at Frank. "I remember helping him a few times before but not on Thursday night."

"That's all right," Frank said soothingly. "I know you were there. And I think there's a good chance you left Montclare's place and boarded some kind of a boat. Does that make any sense?"

"Uhm, well . . . not really," Chrissy replied.

"Maybe just a little?" Jamal said.

"Maybe," Chrissy said, brushing back her hair.

"Good," Joe said.

"Once you boarded the boat," Frank continued, "I think you went out to sea. I know you don't remember, Chrissy, but I want you to try. Close your eyes. Really let yourself relax."

Chrissy shut her eyes and rested her hands on her crossed legs.

"Now listen to the waves," Frank said quietly. "Try to envision yourself on the boat. You're cruising through the dark water. The moon is shaped like a crescent, a little slimmer than it is tonight. After a while I believe you see the *Destiny* in the distance. Your boat is drawing nearer . . . nearer . . . nearer."

Joe saw Chrissy nodding her head slightly, as if following the story. "Is it coming back to you at all?" Frank asked hopefully.

"Maybe it is," Chrissy answered. "Maybe it isn't. I just can't . . . I can't quite get there."

"Keep relaxing," Frank urged. "Stay calm. You're doing just great."

"Chrissy," Joe said softly, "does the word *plutonium* mean anything to you?"

"Plutonium," Chrissy said slowly, her eyes still closed. Then she gave a slight shudder. "The word scares me for some reason, but I'm not sure why."

"Do you remember anything about there being plutonium on Skeleton Reef?" Jamal asked.

"Uh . . ." Chrissy said, her brow wrinkling.

"It was plutonium that sank thirty years ago on a Cuban fishing boat," Frank said, sensing Chrissy was getting close to a memory. "On the northern end of Skeleton Reef. I think you might have known something about the plutonium. And I think this might have had something to do with why someone tried to kill you."

Chrissy shut her eyes tight.

"Come on, Chrissy," Jamal said humorously. "How many Cuban fishing boats are carrying plutonium?"

"Ahh!" Chrissy said, slapping the sand with her hand. "It sounds so familiar but . . . It's like having a word on the tip of your tongue yet not being able to remember it. It's . . . terribly frustrating."

"I bet it is," Frank said sympathetically.

"I want to know what happened to me!" Chrissy said, opening her eyes. "I know someone tried to kill me Thursday night, and I want to know who it was. Then maybe I can find a way to stop them from trying it again. Otherwise I'm going to be on the run for the rest of my life, always living in fear, always looking over my shoulder."

"Take it easy," Joe said, touching Chrissy. "We're going to help you get to the bottom of this."

"Okay," Frank said, trying to collect his thoughts. "The word *plutonium* seemed to ring a bell for Chrissy. I think the plutonium must be why some people are taking the *Destiny* to the northern section of Skeleton Reef. These people tried to murder Chrissy because she knew about it. In fact, I think Chrissy was thrown from the *Destiny* into Skeleton Reef so she would drown. That's why she kept saying 'skeh' right after we found her."

"The problem is," Jamal said, "we'll never be able to prove someone tried to murder Chrissy unless she can remember it. Even if we were to find the culprit, he or she would just deny it, and Chrissy would be in no position to argue."

"It turns out," Frank said, stretching his long legs in the sand, "the biggest secret on Skeleton Reef is the one inside Chrissy Peters's mind."

"I'm sorry," Chrissy said, on the verge of tears. "Really, I'm sorry."

"Forget it," Jamal said, waving a hand. "Well, maybe that's a bad choice of words."

Chrissy smiled. It was the first time Joe had seen her smile, and it made him happy.

"You know," Frank said thoughtfully. "Sometimes when psychiatrists want to help a patient remember an incident that's been blocked out, the psychiatrist takes the person to the place of the incident through hypnosis. Unfortunately we can't do that. But maybe, Chrissy, if we took you to the actual site of the attempted murder, it would help you unlock the secret."

"You could be right," Chrissy said. "It seemed to help a bit just being here on the beach."

"Let's do it tonight," Joe said eagerly. "The longer we delay, the more chance something will happen to Chrissy. Odds are the *Destiny* will be on the northern part of the Reef in a few hours. Just as it was last night."

"Aren't you forgetting a small detail?" Jamal said. "Like the bad guys will be there, too? Some of them might be in the water, but Isaac and Ishmael will probably be on deck. And somehow I doubt they're going to give us a nice friendly welcome."

"I'm getting an interesting idea," Frank said, staring at Chrissy's white caftan.

"What?" Joe asked.

"No, forget it," Frank said, brushing sand off his knee. "It's way too risky."

"Tell us, please," Chrissy said, grabbing Frank's arm. "I have to know what happened to me!"

A wooden skiff was cruising through the sea several hours later with the Hardys, Jamal, and Chrissy aboard. A slender crescent of moon glowed in the sky, but otherwise the sea was quite dark.

Joe and Jamal were both wearing scuba gear, Frank was dressed in black, and Chrissy had applied white makeup all over her face, giving her skin a ghostly pallor. She manned the outboard engine while Frank did the navigating. The skiff had been borrowed from a neighbor of Jamal's uncle.

"I see the *Destiny*," Joe said, peering through

binoculars. "Isaac and Ishmael are on deck, leaning on the starboard gunwale. I don't see anyone else, but there's a faint light in the water."

"That means someone is diving," Jamal said.

"All right," Frank said as Chrissy cut off the outboard. "Let's get this show on the road. Is everybody ready?"

"I guess so," Chrissy said nervously.

"Let's go for it," Jamal said. He and Joe both strapped on diving tanks. Then they put in their mouthpieces, activated their diving watches, and slipped quietly into the water.

With a pair of oars Frank began rowing the skiff toward the *Destiny,* which was still too far away to see without binoculars. "How do I look?" Chrissy asked, moving to the front of the boat.

"Mess your hair up a little," Frank suggested. "Remember, you're supposed to be a ghost who's been dead a few hundred years."

Several minutes later the skiff was nearing the *Destiny.* "Ahoy there!" Isaac called out. "We have exclusive rights to this area! Do not approach!"

Chrissy stood up in the bow of the skiff as Frank continued rowing. Frank saw the giant Ishmael move away from the gunwale as if to fetch something.

"I repeat," Isaac called, "we have exclusive rights to this site. Do not approach!" But Frank kept rowing, the steady rhythm of the oars propelling the skiff forward.

"Maybe you will understand this!" Isaac called. Ishmael handed him a rifle and brought one up to eye level. They took aim at the skiff.

I hope this works, Frank thought. He kept rowing toward the *Destiny*. Chrissy spread her arms, and the white caftan flowed and flapped in the wind.

Isaac and Ishmael lowered their weapons. Frank lifted the oars from the water, letting the skiff float in place.

"Rebecca?" Isaac called out. "Is that you?"

Chrissy stood in the bow, saying nothing.

Isaac and Ishmael stared at Chrissy, and Frank realized they were trying to determine if they were being visited by the fabled ghost of Rebecca. The plan was going well, but Frank knew the two men would not be fooled much longer.

Then, behind Isaac and Ishmael, Joe and Jamal climbed onto the *Destiny*. After removing their fins, they each pulled a length of rope from their weight belt. As Isaac and Ishmael whispered to each other, Joe and Jamal crept up behind them.

Jamal grabbed the arms of Isaac, and Joe grabbed Ishmael's. Before the men could resist, the boys were lashing the ropes around their wrists.

"What is this?" Isaac snarled. "Who are you?"

"What's the matter, guys?" Jamal said. "You two look like you've seen a ghost."

Moving quickly, Joe and Jamal tied their ropes to lashing knobs on the gunwale, binding the islanders to the side of the boat. Then Joe tossed the two rifles into the water. "You can never tell when a gun will be used against you," he told Jamal.

As the men yanked furiously at their ropes, Frank rowed hurriedly toward the *Destiny*. After lashing the skiff to the boat, Frank and Chrissy climbed aboard it. Chrissy ran up to the bridge and started the engine.

Frank, Joe, and Jamal each ran to an anchor point and activated the motors that hauled up the anchors. "Go!" Frank called when the anchors were clear of the water. Chrissy piloted the boat forward a short distance.

From their anchor posts, Frank, Joe, and Jamal looked over the starboard side of the boat, where the water was glimmering turquoise from the diving lights on the sea floor. Soon two heads with scuba masks popped out of the water. Joe recognized them as *Destiny* crew members: Vines, the one with a beard, and Wilson, the one with a mustache.

"What's going on?" Wilson called to the *Destiny*.

"Why are you moving the boat?" Vines shouted.

"Why don't *you* tell us!" Joe yelled back.

The two divers looked startled when they spied newcomers on the boat.

"Those boys!" Isaac shouted, still tied to the gunwale. "They have pirated the boat! And they have Chrissy Peters with them!"

Chrissy screamed in terror.

Frank heard someone climbing onto the boat

right behind him, but before he could turn, a muscular arm wrapped tightly around his chest. When Frank saw an anchor tattoo on the giant biceps, he realized the person holding him was Lou Brunelli.

Brunelli pressed the cold blade of a diving knife against Frank's throat. "Nobody make a move," he called out. "If you do, brother Frank here gets his head cut off!"

15 The Truth Surfaces

With the sharp blade of the knife only inches from his jugular, Frank didn't dare to even blink an eye.

"Nobody is moving," Jamal said, holding a calm hand in the air. "Everything is real cool."

"Come out of the water!" Brunelli called to Vines and Wilson. Brunelli's eyes flashed with focused rage, and Joe realized he was probably the one in charge of the operation. Brunelli was bare-chested, wearing only his tank and the bottom of a wet suit. Wilson and Vines, wearing complete wet suits, swam toward the *Destiny* and climbed aboard.

"Untie Isaac and Ishmael!" Brunelli yelled to Wilson and Vines as he kept his diving knife at Frank's throat. "And get the guns."

"They threw the rifles in the water!" Isaac called from the gunwale.

"Then get the spearguns," Brunelli ordered.

As Wilson and Vines obeyed, Joe looked up at Chrissy on the bridge. She was staring at Brunelli, her eyes wide with recognition. "Chrissy, what is it?" Joe called up to her.

"I remember everything now!" Chrissy exclaimed. "Seeing Lou Brunelli standing there, his eyes glaring like a monster's, it's bringing the whole awful night flooding back to me!"

"I didn't want to hurt you, Chrissy," Brunelli yelled. "I had no choice. You know that, don't you?"

Isaac and Ishmael were freed, and Wilson and Vines were holding loaded spearguns. "What happened?" Joe asked. He was not only trying to stall for time—he also wanted to get to the bottom of the mystery. "Come on. Tell us everything."

"Should we kill them?" Vines asked, fingering the trigger of his speargun.

"Not yet," Brunelli said. "I'm thinking."

"Go on, Chrissy," Joe urged.

"Let me see," Chrissy said, gazing across the calm water. "Some time back, a few weeks ago, Sandy Flask mentioned to Brunelli that a lady had told him there was plutonium somewhere on the northern part of Skeleton Reef. Apparently it went down with a Cuban fishing boat about thirty years ago."

"Keep going, Chrissy," Jamal said.

"The lady wanted Flask to find the plutonium and give it to her," Chrissy continued. "Flask said he would try when his work on the *Laughing Moon* slowed down. But Brunelli decided he wanted to find the plutonium right away."

"Why?" Frank asked, the blade still at his neck.

"He wanted to sell it," Chrissy explained. "He saw this as a quick way to get rich. Then he got Wilson, Vines, Isaac, and Ishmael to help him. They started moving the *Destiny* every night and diving on the northern reef to look for the lost plutonium."

"So how did you get mixed up in this?" Jamal asked Chrissy.

"Go on, Miss Chrissy," Brunelli said. "If you're going to tell the story, tell it all."

"Brunelli and his mates spent a week looking for the plutonium," Chrissy continued. "But apparently they were having a lot of trouble finding it. They wanted an extra hand. A few days ago Brunelli asked if I wanted to join the search. I said yes."

"You sure did," Brunelli said sarcastically. "So don't make out like you're the only innocent one around here, Miss Chrissy!"

"I was awfully broke," Chrissy said, obviously feeling great shame. "Half my meals were just bananas and canned beans. And then, seeing all that beautiful gold every day made me desperate for money. So, yes, I agreed to join them. Thursday night was supposed to be my first night on the job. I helped Pierre Montclare with his bookkeeping that night. Then, when I was done, I met Brunelli and these guys at the harbor. We took a boat out to the *Destiny*, then sailed to the northern end of the reef."

"What happened next?" Joe asked.

"The guys were talking about who they might sell the plutonium to," Chrissy explained. "They mentioned small countries, terrorist groups, right-wing organizations in the U.S. And for the first time I began to realize we would be helping some organization create an atomic bomb. A bomb that could destroy thousands of lives. I realized how terribly wrong this all was."

"So you wanted out," Frank said.

"I told them I couldn't go along," Chrissy said. "I tried to get the others to see how evil this business was, but they were obsessed with the idea. They said they wouldn't stop, and then I noticed they were all looking at me strangely. I felt as if I were surrounded by a tribe of starving cannibals."

"You would have put the whole operation at risk," Wilson called out.

"Brunelli said they couldn't trust me anymore and that they couldn't let me go," Chrissy said, her voice deepening with anger. "Then he pulled out his diving knife and held it to my neck, just as he's doing right now with Frank. Lou Brunelli, this guy who was supposed to be my friend, was going to slit my throat!"

"But I didn't!" Lou shouted. "I didn't slit your throat, did I, Chrissy?"

"No," Chrissy called down from the bridge, her voice ragged with emotion. "You said you couldn't kill someone you knew and liked. Then Isaac aimed the rifle at me, but he couldn't kill me, either. None of them could. Finally Lou said there was only one way to do it. He grabbed me and threw me overboard. I tried to climb back on the boat, but Isaac and Ishmael kept me away with the rifles. You see, they were too gutless to kill me, but they were happy to let me drown in the sea."

"So you swam," Jamal said.

"I had no choice," Chrissy said. "I swam for St. Lucia, hoping I might find a vessel somewhere along the way. But I didn't come across anything so I just kept swimming. I got pretty far, but at some point I conked out."

"And then we found you on the shore," Joe said.

"That's right," Chrissy answered. "The water must have brought me in."

"I had a sneaking feeling you might have made it back alive," Brunelli said. "I just had a feeling."

"You're no dummy, Brunelli," Frank scoffed.

"No, kid, I'm not," Brunelli said, pressing the blade against Frank's neck. "Yesterday evening I stopped by the Soufrière hospital and discovered Chrissy had been there. I also found out there were two teenage boys with her, one blond, one dark haired. Then I remembered all the nosy questions Frank and Joe Hardy were asking on the boat yesterday, and I figured they were the two teenagers."

"So you tried to scare us off the case," Joe said. "You found out where we were staying and tossed the bottle through the window. The black spot was a nice touch, by the way."

"I thought you boys might appreciate that," Brunelli said with a grin. *Treasure Island* was the only book in school I liked."

"And you were also the maniac shooting us with a speargun this afternoon," Frank said.

"Careful who you call a maniac," Brunelli said, nicking Frank's neck with the blade. "But yes, I followed you guys a long time yesterday until I had a shot at you. They were just warning shots, though. I'm not a killer by nature."

"Come on, Lou," Vines asked impatiently. "What are we going to do?"

"It's them or us," Wilson said.

"We have to kill them." Ishmael spoke in a very deep bass voice. "Otherwise we get no plutonium and we maybe go to jail." Joe realized it was the first time he had actually heard Ishmael speak.

"But this time," Isaac said, "we better make sure they're dead *before* we throw them in the water."

"I know, I know, I know!" Brunelli thundered with fury and frustration. "I don't like it, but at this

143

point the only solution I can come up with is to deliver on that black spot. For all four of you."

Over the past few minutes Frank had been searching his mind for a way to untie the deadly knot binding him and his companions. He finally realized a possible answer was staring him right in the face—on Brunelli's tattoo. Frank looked intently in Joe's direction, hoping his brother would notice.

Joe saw Frank staring at him. The Hardys were pretty good at communicating without words, and Joe was trying to figure out what exactly Frank had in mind. Frank glanced at the anchor tattoo on Brunelli's biceps, then at the anchor line running right near his feet.

Joe got it. He nodded slightly at Frank.

Frank took a step forward and kicked the anchor lever. The motor whirred, hauling anchor line into the boat. "Watch it!" Brunelli said, moving forward with Frank, thinking he was trying to escape.

But Joe was right there. He stopped the lever, waited, then pulled the lever in the other direction.

"Ahhhh!" Brunelli screamed as a loop of slack rope tightened around his ankle. The knife clattered onto the deck, and Brunelli was jerked off his feet by the uncoiling rope, then dragged across the deck.

Joe pushed in the lever. The line stopped pulling Brunelli but was still biting into his ankle. "Owww, that hurts!" Brunelli yelled, trying in vain to loosen the rope from his leg.

144

"Drop the spearguns and jump overboard!" Joe shouted. "All of you! As soon as you're in, we'll free Brunelli!" Wilson, Vines, and the two islanders hesitated.

"Drop the spearguns and jump!" Joe repeated. "Otherwise your friend here might lose a leg. Don't worry, we're not going to let you die."

"Do it!" Brunelli screamed in pain. "Now!"

"But, Lou—" Wilson began.

"Please!" Brunelli yelled in agony. "Jump!"

Wilson and Vine dropped their spearguns on the deck and jumped into the water. Isaac and Ishmael splashed in after them.

Joe immediately hauled some anchor line back in, allowing Brunelli to free his leg. Frank realized Brunelli's injury probably would not be too bad since the man's ankles were covered by the wet suit.

"Sorry about this," Joe said as he and Frank grabbed the injured Brunelli and heaved him overboard. But as he fell, Brunelli grabbed Frank's arm and pulled him into the water with him. At once, Isaac and Ishmael raced over to Frank and pushed him underwater.

"That's it for him," Vines said, treading water.

Jamal picked up the two spearguns and handed one to Joe. The two boys lowered their masks, inserted their mouthpieces, and leaped into the water.

As his weight belt pulled him downward, Joe

looked around. Through the eerie, shimmering glow of the diving lights, Joe saw Isaac and Ishmael holding Frank down. Isaac and Ishmael's cheeks were puffed out, and Joe could see they had been prepared to hold their breaths. Frank, however, had been caught off guard and was desperately in need of air.

Joe aimed his speargun at Ishmael, then pulled the trigger. A spear sailed swiftly through the clear water and ripped through Ishmael's pants. The giant released Frank to pull the spear from his leg. Then Frank kicked Isaac in the chest, freed himself, and swam madly for the surface.

A hand ripped out Joe's mouthpiece. As Joe clamped his mouth shut, Lou Brunelli grabbed him by the shoulders and spun him around. Brunelli was drawing breath from a tank, but Joe had only seconds of air stored in his own lungs.

Joe drove the butt of the speargun into Brunelli's chest, but with one hand Brunelli yanked the gun away and tossed it. Glancing around, Joe saw Jamal skirmishing with the other bad guys in the watery distance. Frank was nowhere in sight. As Brunelli kept holding him, second after long second, Joe felt his eyes start to bulge from lack of oxygen.

Brunelli continued holding Joe with a viselike grip around his throat.

Joe felt his lungs were about to explode!

Dizzy and disoriented, Joe glimpsed a swarm of scarlet fish below. No, the scarlet wasn't fish, it was coral, he dimly realized. Joe knew he couldn't free himself from Brunelli's powerful grasp, but he had an idea. With a burst of strength, he shoved Brunelli downward.

Brunelli let go of Joe, his face distorted with pain as his bare back scraped against the sharp coral. Joe quickly kicked his way to the surface.

Frank saw Joe swimming up as he swam down to help Jamal, who was now surrounded by Wilson, Vines, Isaac, and Ishmael. Jamal shot his last spear, catching Wilson in the fin. As the others converged on Jamal, Frank swam into the fray, holding everyone back with a freshly loaded speargun Chrissy had just handed him from the deck of the *Destiny.*

Frank pointed downward, indicating he wanted all the bad guys to descend farther. Fearing the speargun's vengeance, the four villains descended as Frank and Jamal shot upward for the surface.

Frank and Jamal broke through the water, then called to Joe, who was about to go down again. The three boys clambered aboard the *Destiny,* brought up the anchors, and Chrissy began piloting the boat away. The five bad guys popped out of the water like corks.

"Wait!" Vines screamed. "Don't leave us out here! We'll never make it! We've only got minutes of air in our tanks!"

"Have a heart!" Wilson shouted. "Please."

"Now you know how it feels!" Chrissy yelled down from the bridge. "Pretty scary, isn't it?"

147

"I'm sorry, Chrissy!" Brunelli cried out.

"Shut up and start treading water!" Joe yelled to the frightened men. "We'll radio for a police boat to pick you up. After they get you in handcuffs, you can tell them your side of the story."

Soon the *Destiny* was out of hearing range of the screaming villains. Chrissy had radioed the police, and a boat was on the way to haul them in. As the *Destiny* plowed through the calm Caribbean Sea, Joe and Jamal stood with Chrissy up on the bridge. Joe glanced up at the glowing crescent moon, finally feeling his adrenaline level return to normal.

"You know," Chrissy said, her chestnut hair dancing in the wind, "Sandy Flask was right. The scent of treasure does change people. It even happened to me. But I've learned my lesson, and I have a lot to thank you guys for."

"Now," Jamal said with a smile, "maybe I can get the Hardy brothers to take it easy for a few days."

"That's exactly what I have in mind," Joe said, squeezing Jamal's arm. Joe noticed Frank below, leaning on the port gunwale, watching the dark water flow by. Joe climbed down from the bridge and approached his older brother.

"What are you thinking?" Joe asked.

"Oh, nothing," Frank replied.

"Nope," Joe said. "I can tell you're thinking about something. Tell me what it is."

"Okay," Frank said, his brown eyes turning mischievous. "I was just wondering what other secrets might lie buried out there on Skeleton Reef. There's bound to be a few more."

"Well, if you find anything," Joe said, pointing a stern finger at Frank, "keep it to yourself. Starting right now, I am officially on vacation."

NANCY DREW® MYSTERY STORIES By Carolyn Keene

A MINSTREL® BOOK
Published by Pocket Books

**Do your younger brothers and sisters
want to read books like yours?**

**Let them know there
are books just for *them*!**

They can join Nancy Drew and her best
friends as they collect clues and solve
mysteries in

THE NANCY DREW NOTEBOOKS

Starting with
#1 The Slumber Party Secret
#2 The Lost Locket

AND

**Meet up with suspense and mystery
in Frank and Joe Hardy:
The Clues Brothers™**

#1 The Gross Ghost Mystery
#2 The Karate Clue

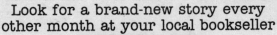

Look for a brand-new story every
other month at your local bookseller

A MINSTREL® BOOK

Published by Pocket Books   1366

Sometimes, it takes a kid to solve a good crime....

Original stories based on the hit Nickelodeon show!

#1 A Slash in the Night
by Alan Goodman

#2 Takeout Stakeout
By Diana G. Gallagher

(Coming in mid-June 1997)

#3 Rock 'n' Roll Robbery
by Lydia C. Marano and David Cody Weiss

(Coming in mid-August 1997)

#4 Hot Rock
by John Peel

(Coming in mid-October 1997)

To find out more about *The Mystery Files of Shelby Woo* or any other Nickelodeon show, visit Nickelodeon Online on America Online (Keyword: NICK) or send e-mail (NickMailDD@aol.com).

A MINSTREL BOOK

Published by Pocket Books

THE HARDY BOYS® SERIES By Franklin W. Dixon